Emmanuel Guibert   Marc Boutavant

ARIOL

Happy as a Pig...

PAPERCUTZ™

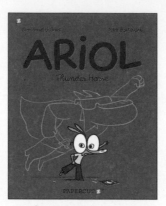

Happy as a Pig...

To Mrs. Nays,
– Emmanuel Guibert

ARIOL
#3 Happy as a Pig...

Emmanuel Guibert – Writer
Marc Boutavant – Artist
Rémi Chaurand – Colorist
Joe Johnson – Translation
Michael Petranek – Lettering
Beth Scorzato – Production Coordinator
Michael Petranek – Associate Editor
Jim Salicrup
Editor-in-Chief

Volume 3: Copain comme Cochon © Bayard Editions –– 2011

ISBN: 978-1-59707-487-2

Printed in China
December 2013 by New Era Printing, LTD.
Unit C. 8/F Worldwide Centre
123 Chung Tau, Kowloon
Hong Kong

Papercutz books may be purchased for business or promotional use. For information on bulk purchases please
contact Macmillan Corporate and Premium Sales Department at (800) 221-7945 x5442.

Distributed by Macmillan
First Papercutz Printing

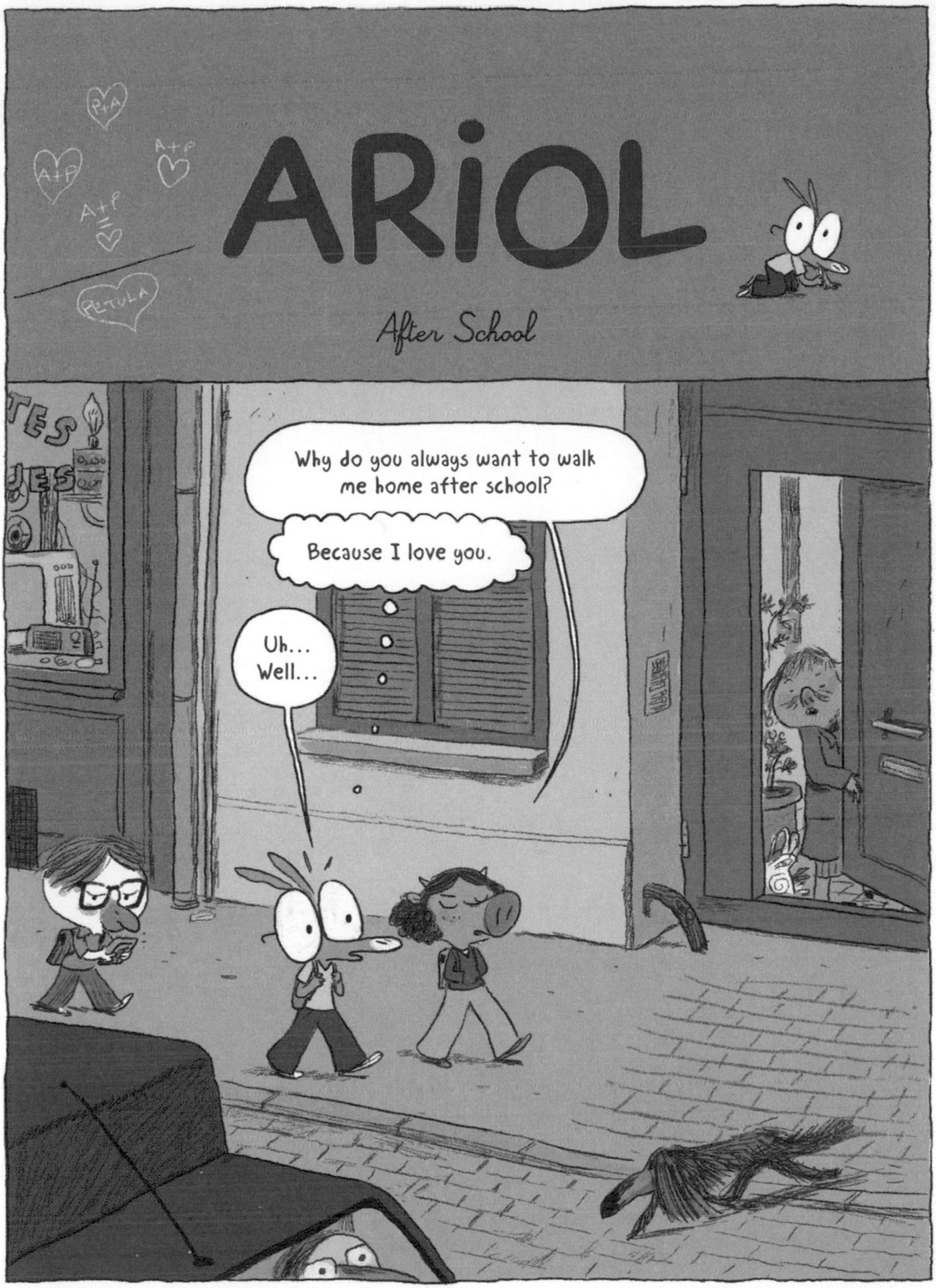
P+A
A+P
A+P
A+P =
PETULA
ARiOL
After School
Why do you always want to walk me home after school?
Because I love you.
Uh... Well...

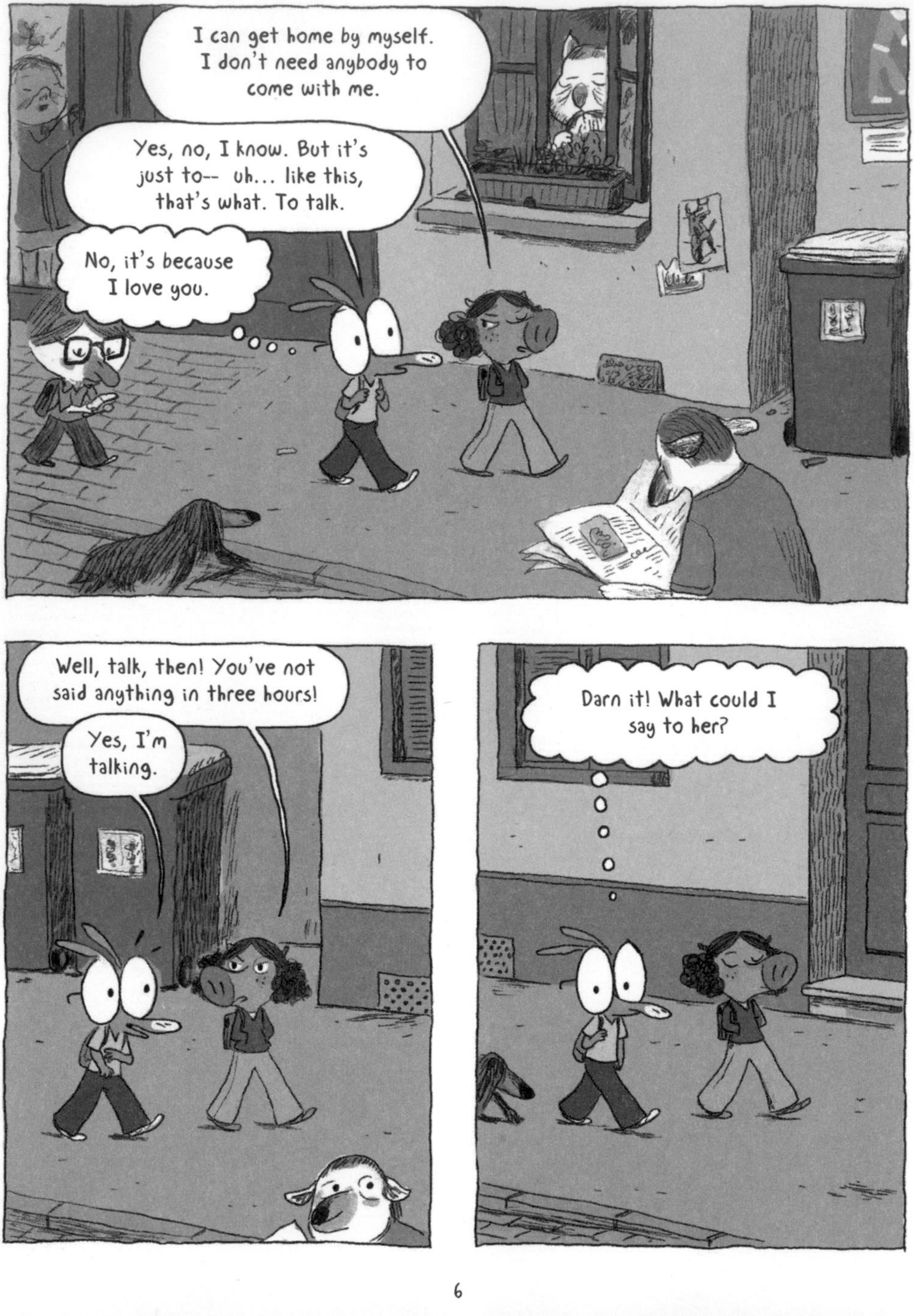

I can get home by myself. I don't need anybody to come with me.
Yes, no, I know. But it's just to-- uh... like this, that's what. To talk.
No, it's because I love you.
Well, talk, then! You've not said anything in three hours!
Yes, I'm talking.
Darn it! What could I say to her?

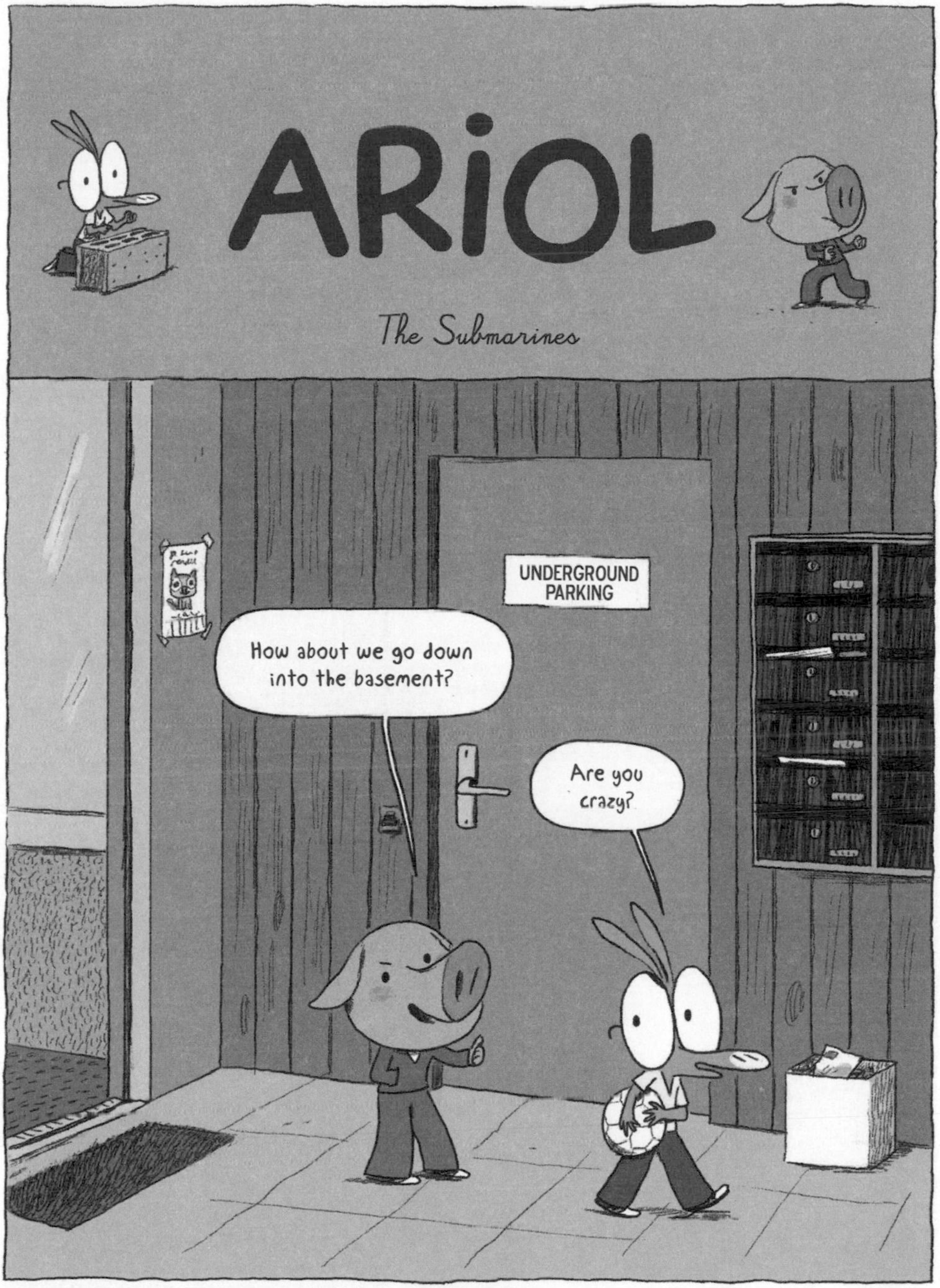
ARiOL
The Submarines
UNDERGROUND PARKING
How about we go down into the basement?
Are you crazy?

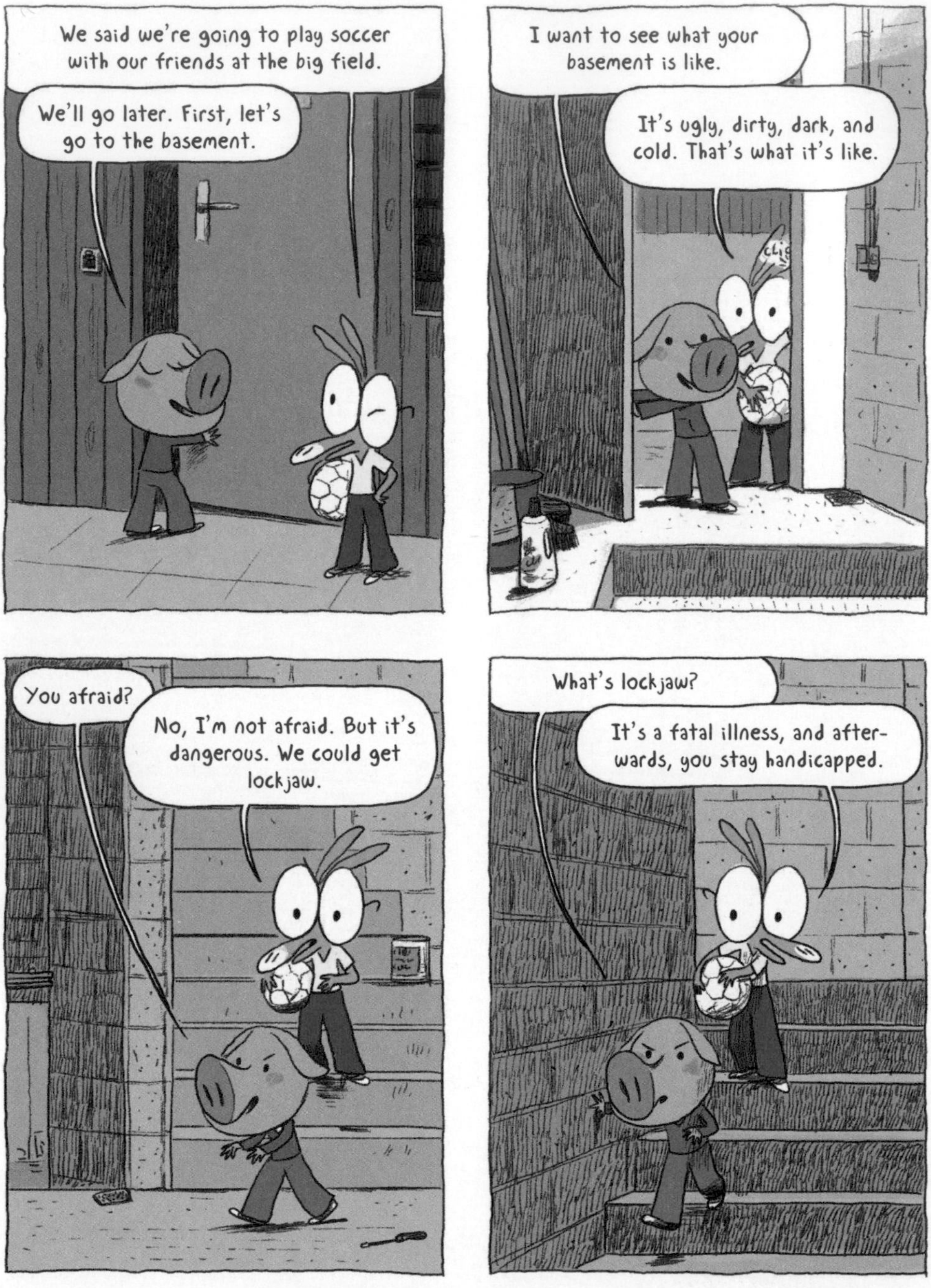
We said we're going to play soccer with our friends at the big field.
We'll go later. First, let's go to the basement.
I want to see what your basement is like.
It's ugly, dirty, dark, and cold. That's what it's like.
You afraid?
No, I'm not afraid. But it's dangerous. We could get lockjaw.
What's lockjaw?
It's a fatal illness, and after-wards, you stay handicapped.

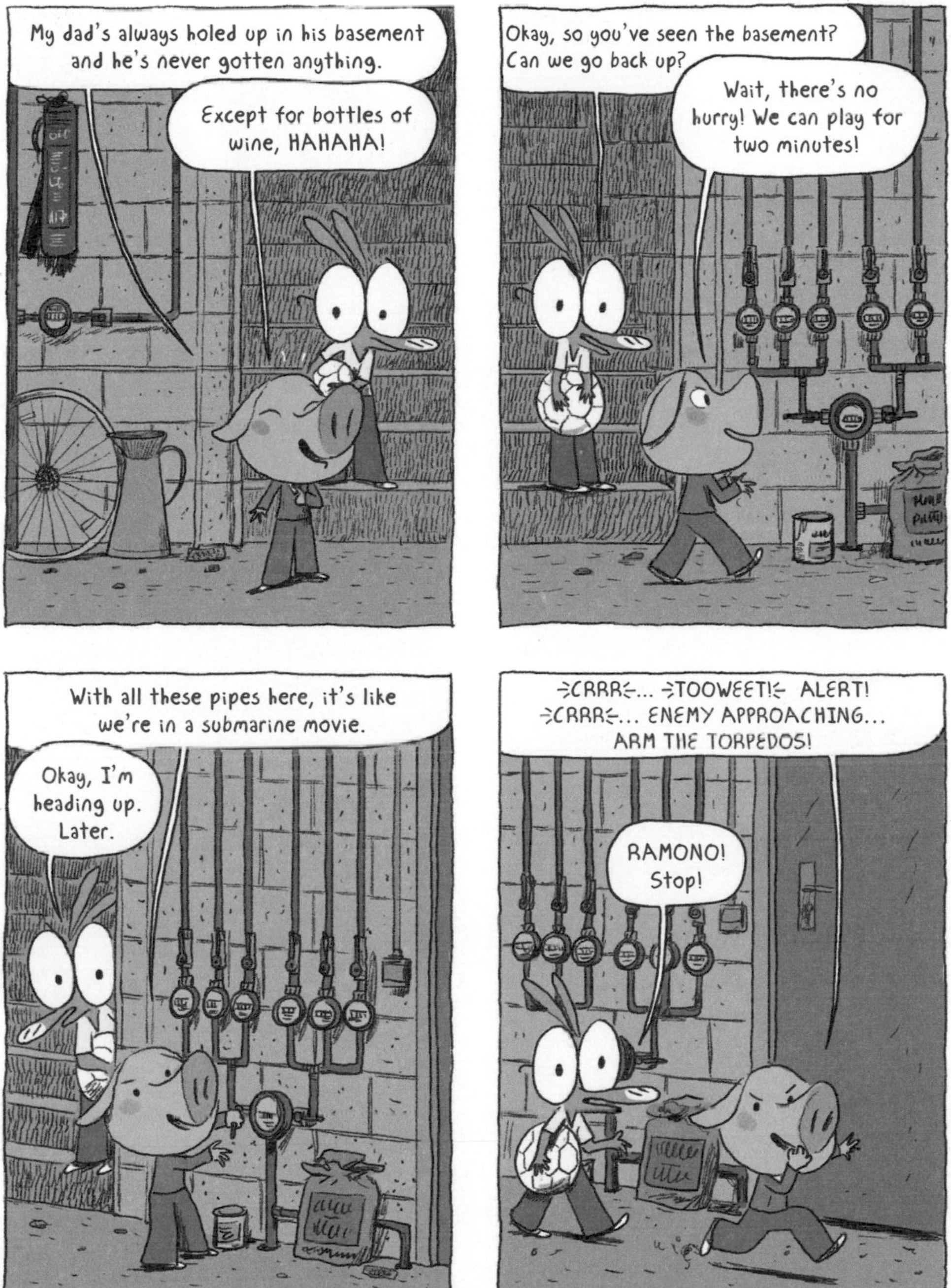
My dad's always holed up in his basement and he's never gotten anything.
Except for bottles of wine, HAHAHA!
Okay, so you've seen the basement? Can we go back up?
Wait, there's no hurry! We can play for two minutes!
With all these pipes here, it's like we're in a submarine movie.
Okay, I'm heading up. Later.
=CRRR=... =TOOWEET!= ALERT! =CRRR=... ENEMY APPROACHING... ARM THE TORPEDOS!
RAMONO! Stop!

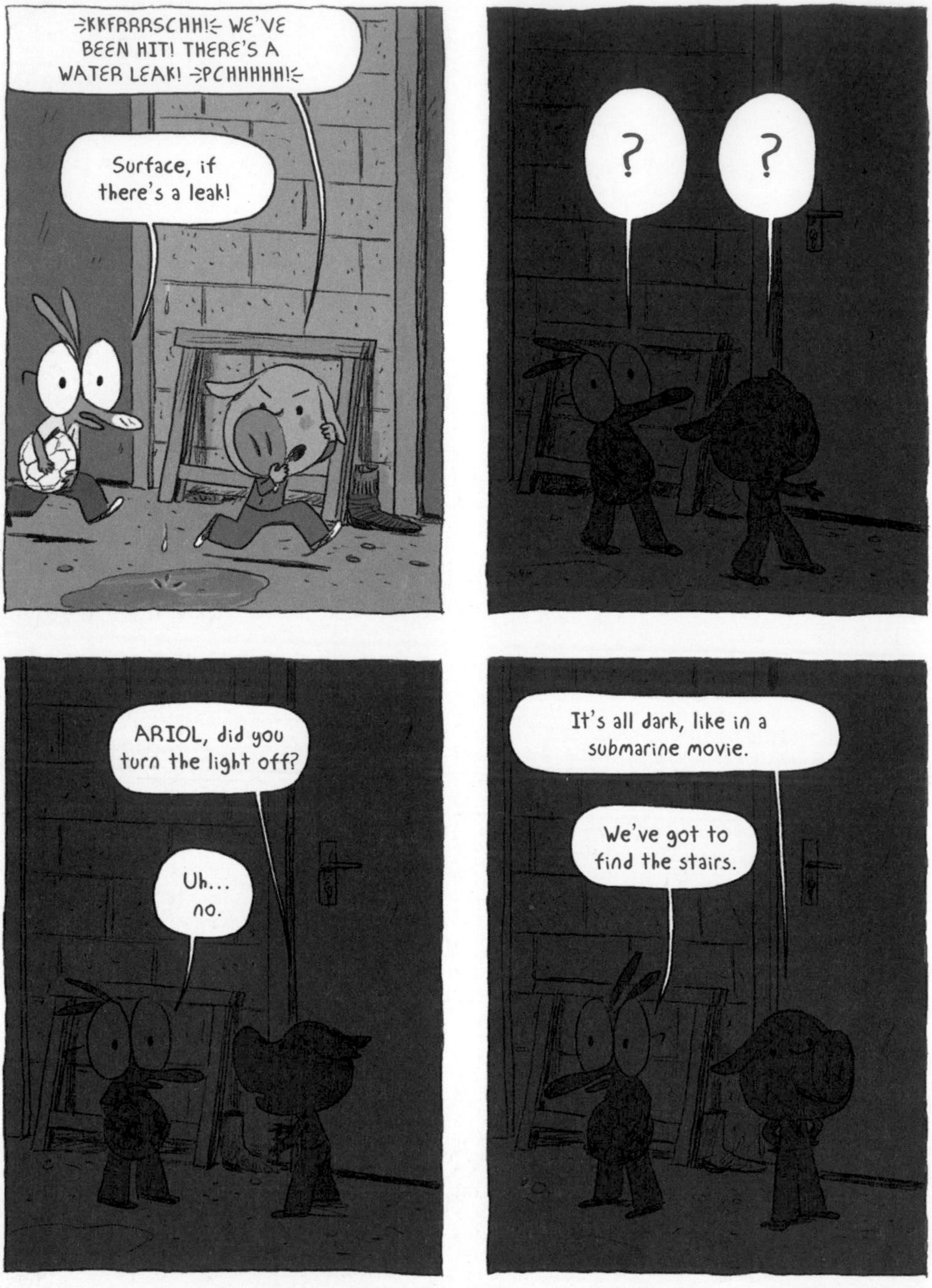
⇒KKFRRRSCHH!⇐ WE'VE BEEN HIT! THERE'S A WATER LEAK! ⇒PCHHHHH!⇐
Surface, if there's a leak!
?
?
ARIOL, did you turn the light off?
Uh... no.
It's all dark, like in a submarine movie.
We've got to find the stairs.

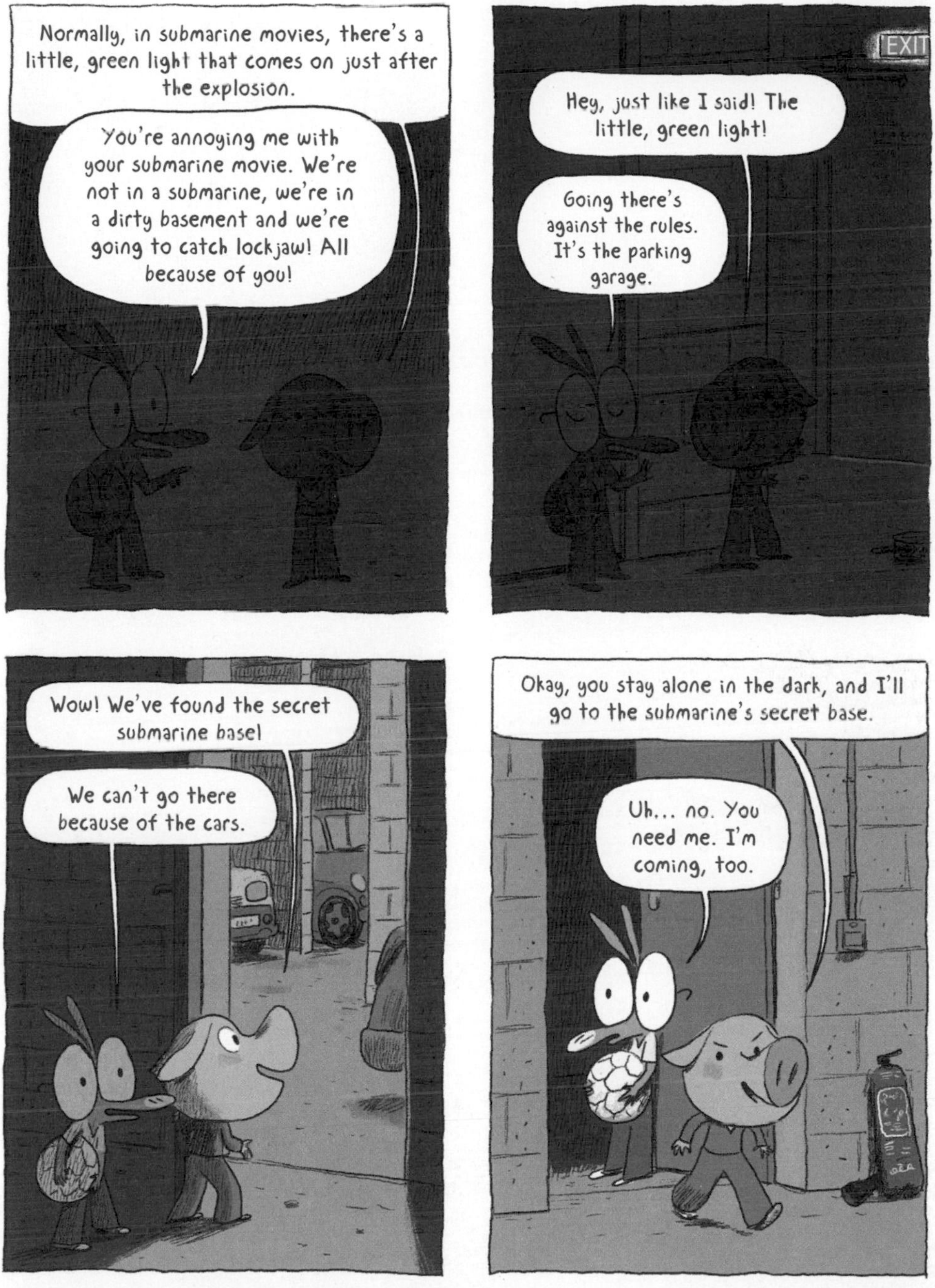
Normally, in submarine movies, there's a little, green light that comes on just after the explosion.
You're annoying me with your submarine movie. We're not in a submarine, we're in a dirty basement and we're going to catch lockjaw! All because of you!
EXIT
Hey, just like I said! The little, green light!
Going there's against the rules. It's the parking garage.
Wow! We've found the secret submarine base!
We can't go there because of the cars.
Okay, you stay alone in the dark, and I'll go to the submarine's secret base.
Uh... no. You need me. I'm coming, too.

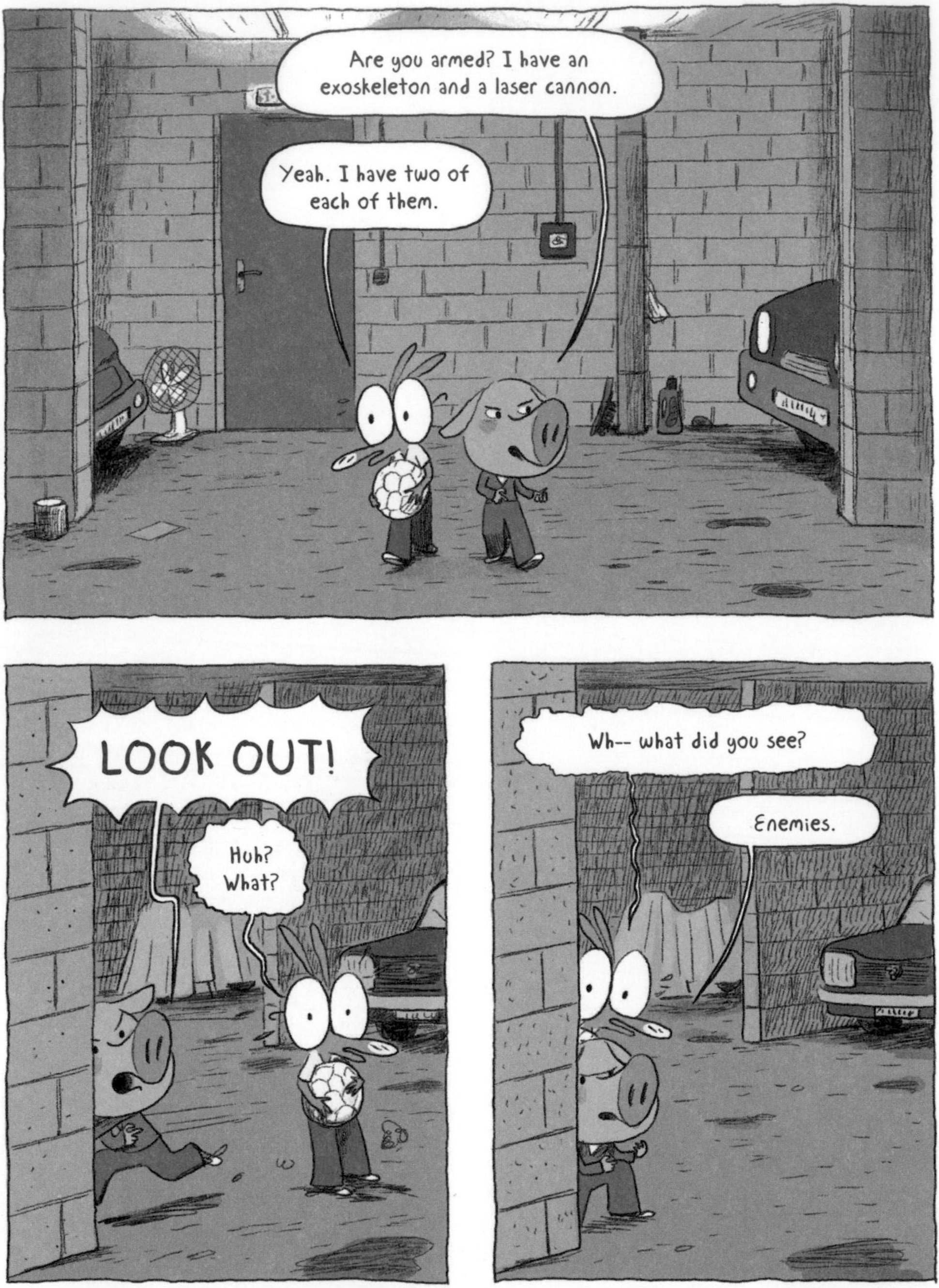

Are you armed? I have an exoskeleton and a laser cannon.
Yeah. I have two of each of them.
LOOK OUT!
Huh? What?
Wh-- what did you see?
Enemies.

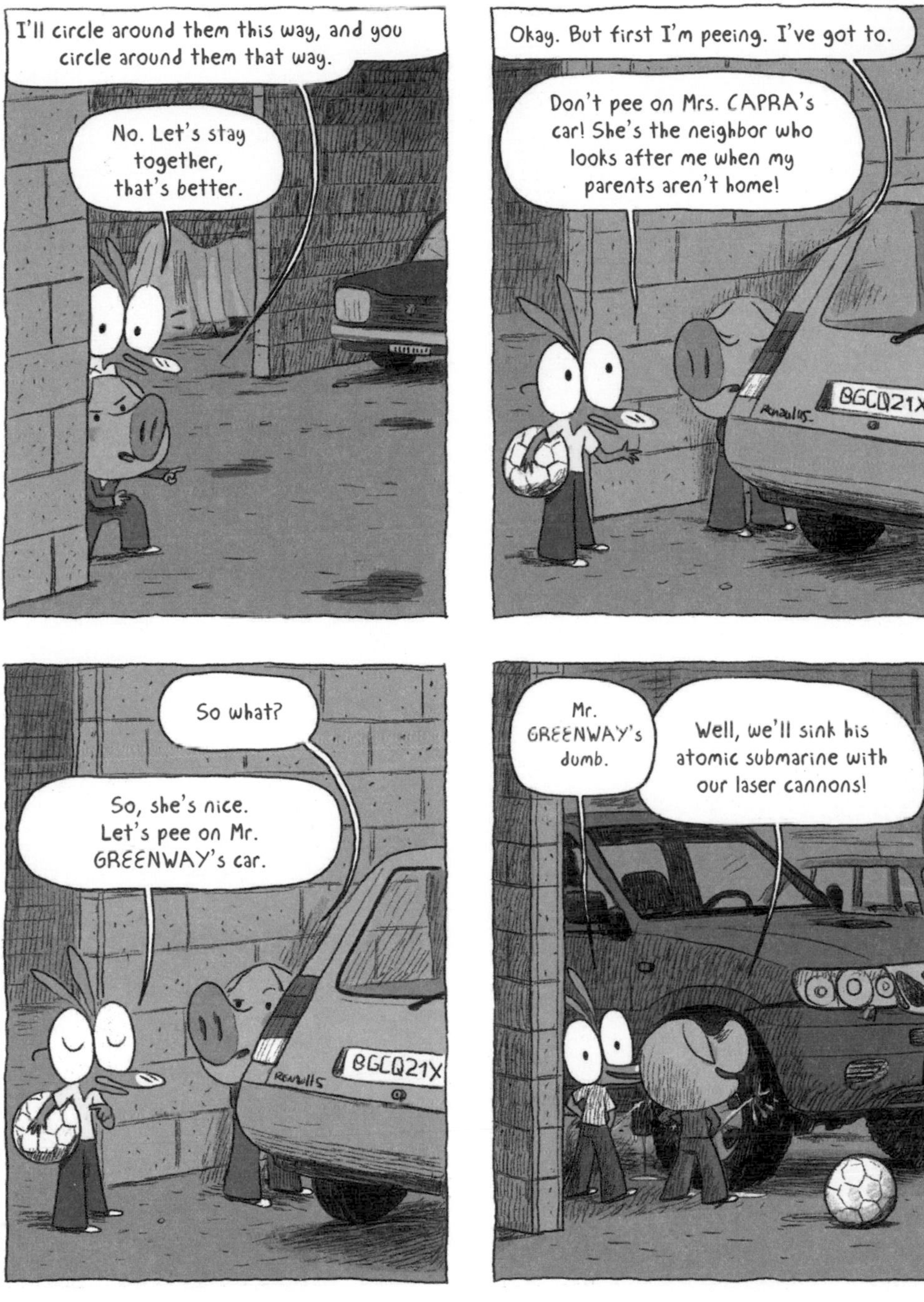
I'll circle around them this way, and you circle around them that way.
No. Let's stay together, that's better.
Okay. But first I'm peeing. I've got to.
Don't pee on Mrs. CAPRA's car! She's the neighbor who looks after me when my parents aren't home!
BGCQ21X
So what?
So, she's nice. Let's pee on Mr. GREENWAY's car.
BGCQ21X
Mr. GREENWAY's dumb.
Well, we'll sink his atomic submarine with our laser cannons!

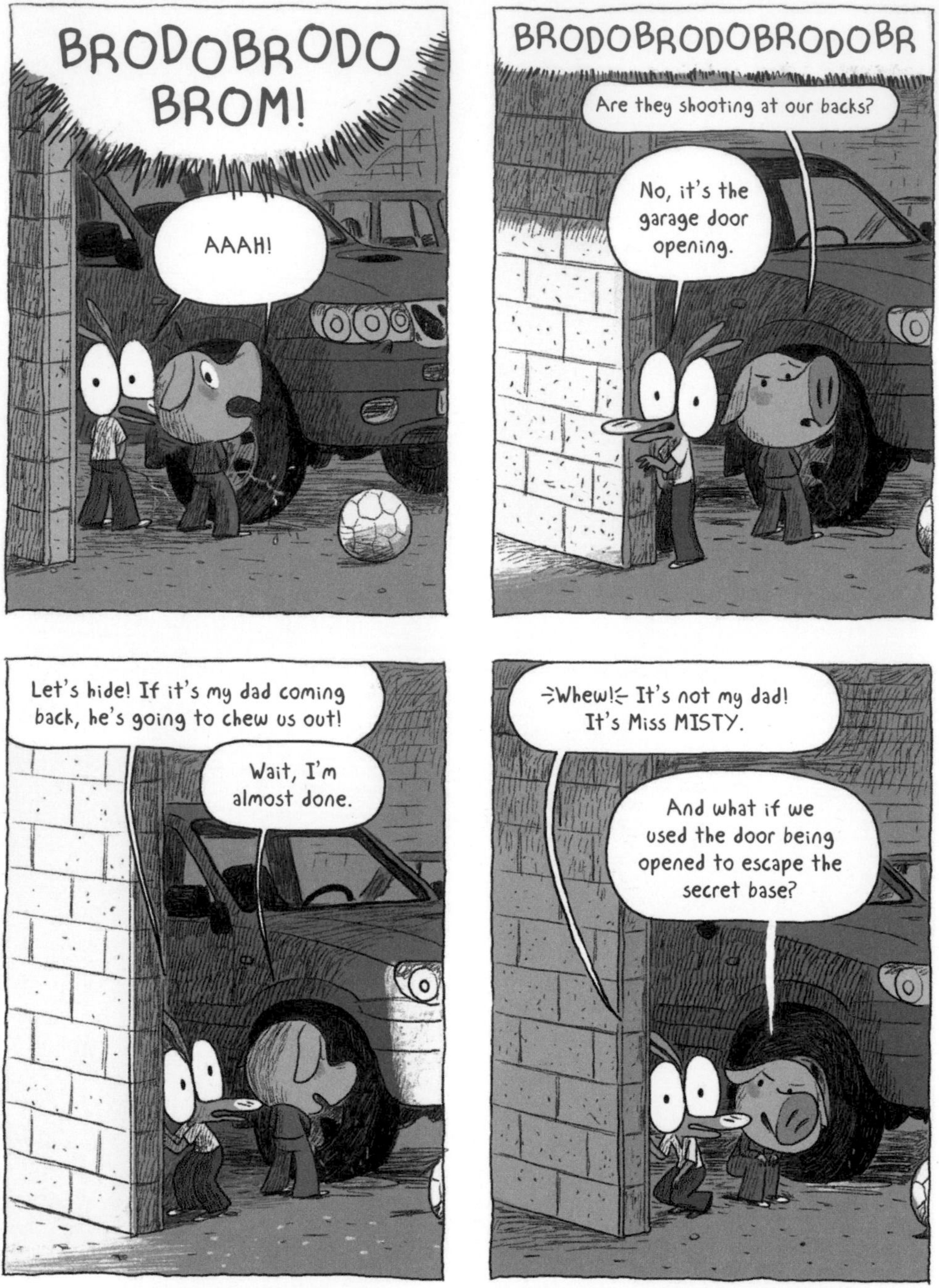
BRODOBRODO BROM!
AAAH!
BRODOBRODOBRODOBR
Are they shooting at our backs?
No, it's the garage door opening.
Let's hide! If it's my dad coming back, he's going to chew us out!
Wait, I'm almost done.
Whew! It's not my dad! It's Miss MISTY.
And what if we used the door being opened to escape the secret base?

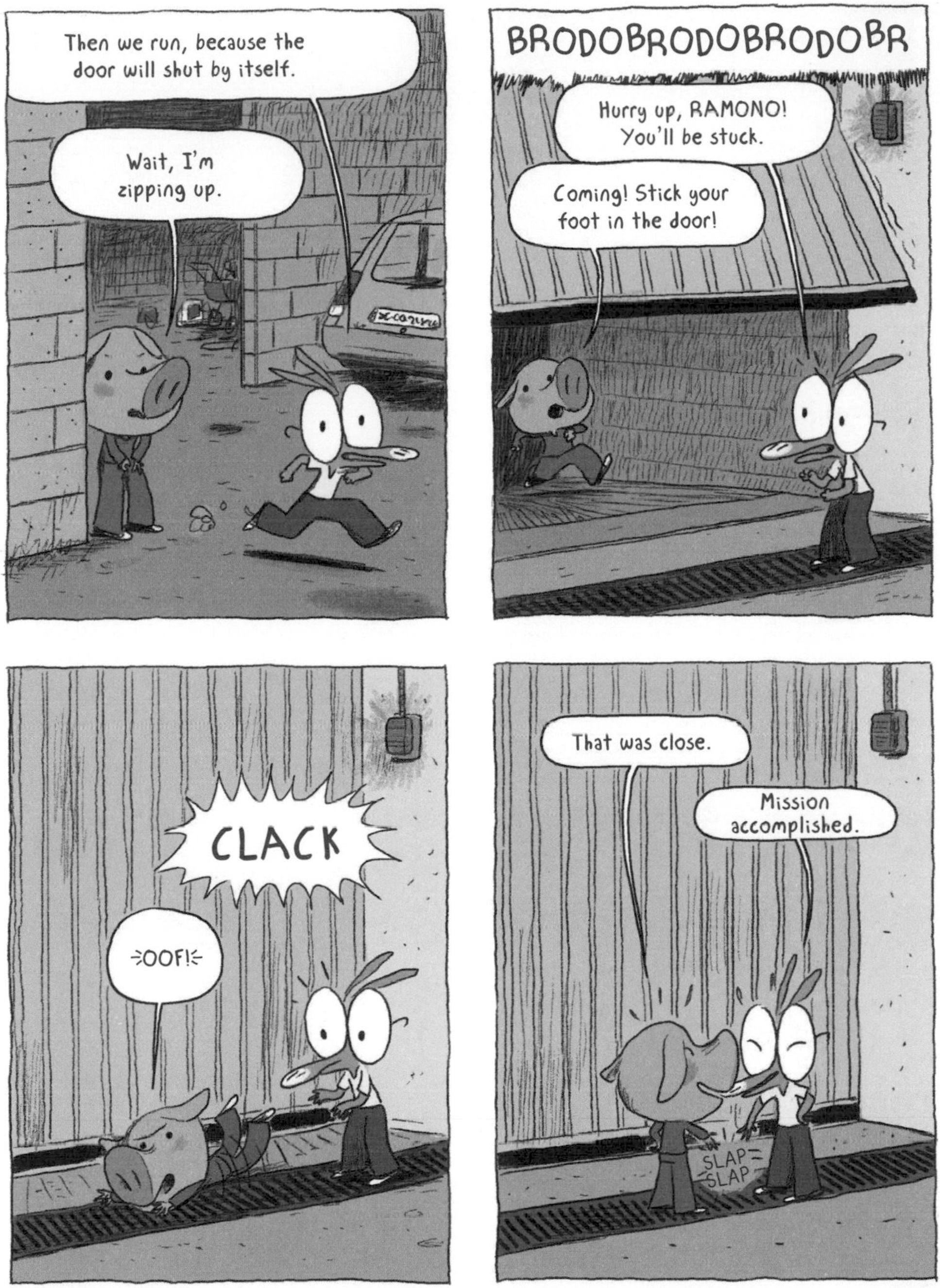
Then we run, because the door will shut by itself.
Wait, I'm zipping up.
BRODOBRODOBRODOBR
Hurry up, RAMONO! You'll be stuck.
Coming! Stick your foot in the door!
CLACK
OOF!
That was close.
Mission accomplished.
SLAP SLAP

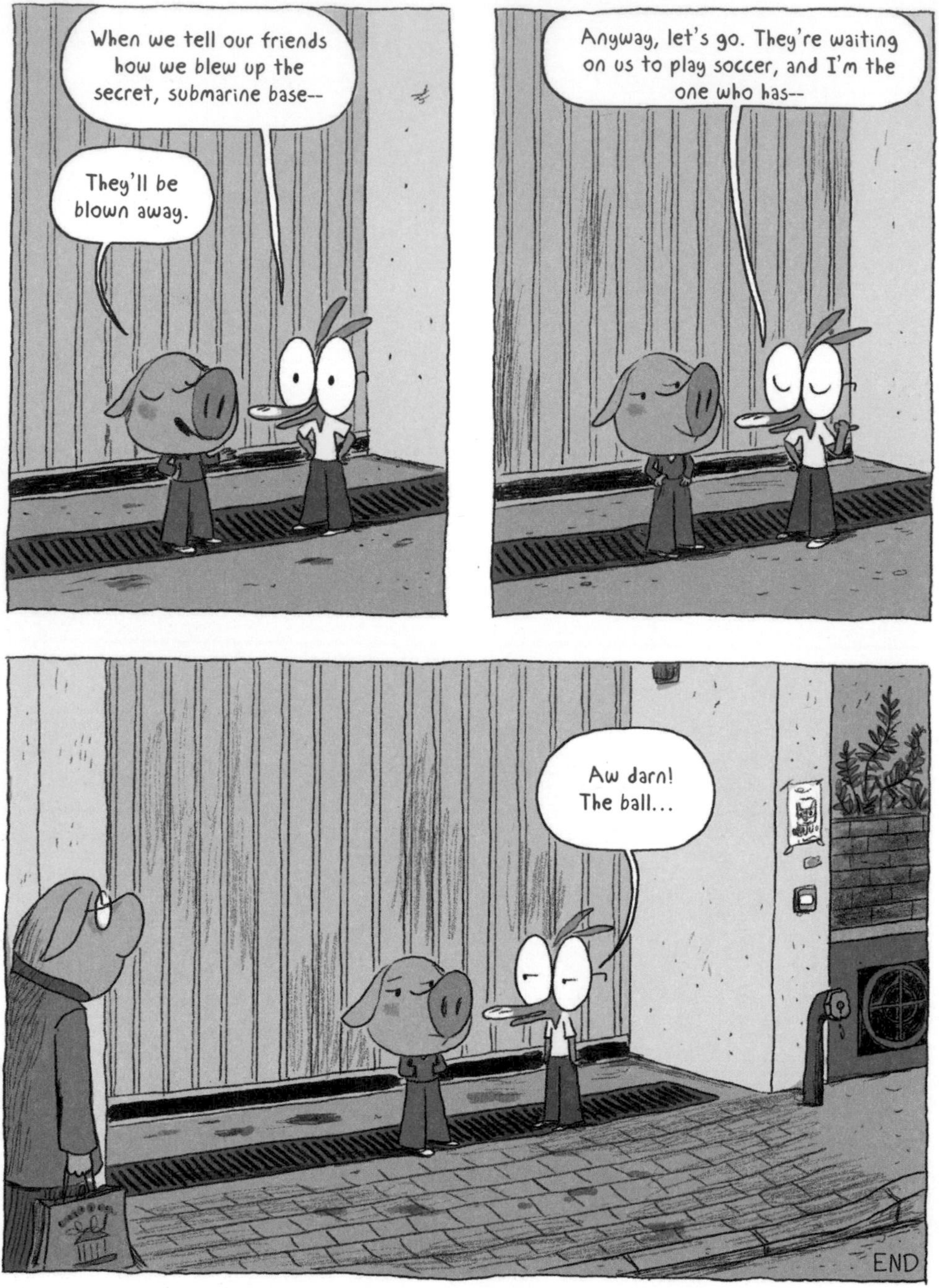
When we tell our friends how we blew up the secret, submarine base--
They'll be blown away.
Anyway, let's go. They're waiting on us to play soccer, and I'm the one who has--
Aw darn! The ball...
END

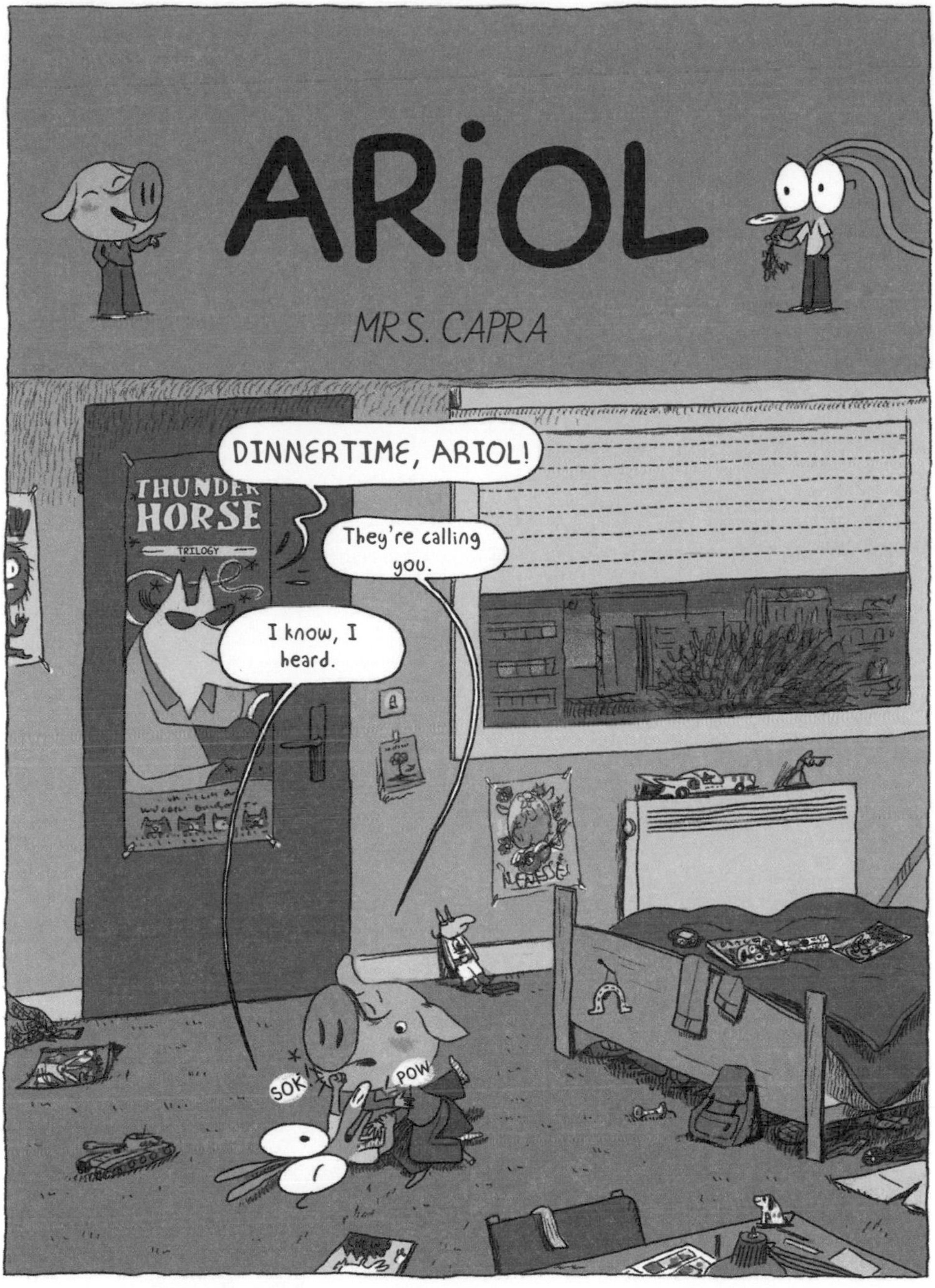
ARiOL
MRS. CAPRA
DINNERTIME, ARIOL!
They're calling you.
I know, I heard.
THUNDER HORSE
TRILOGY
SOK
POW

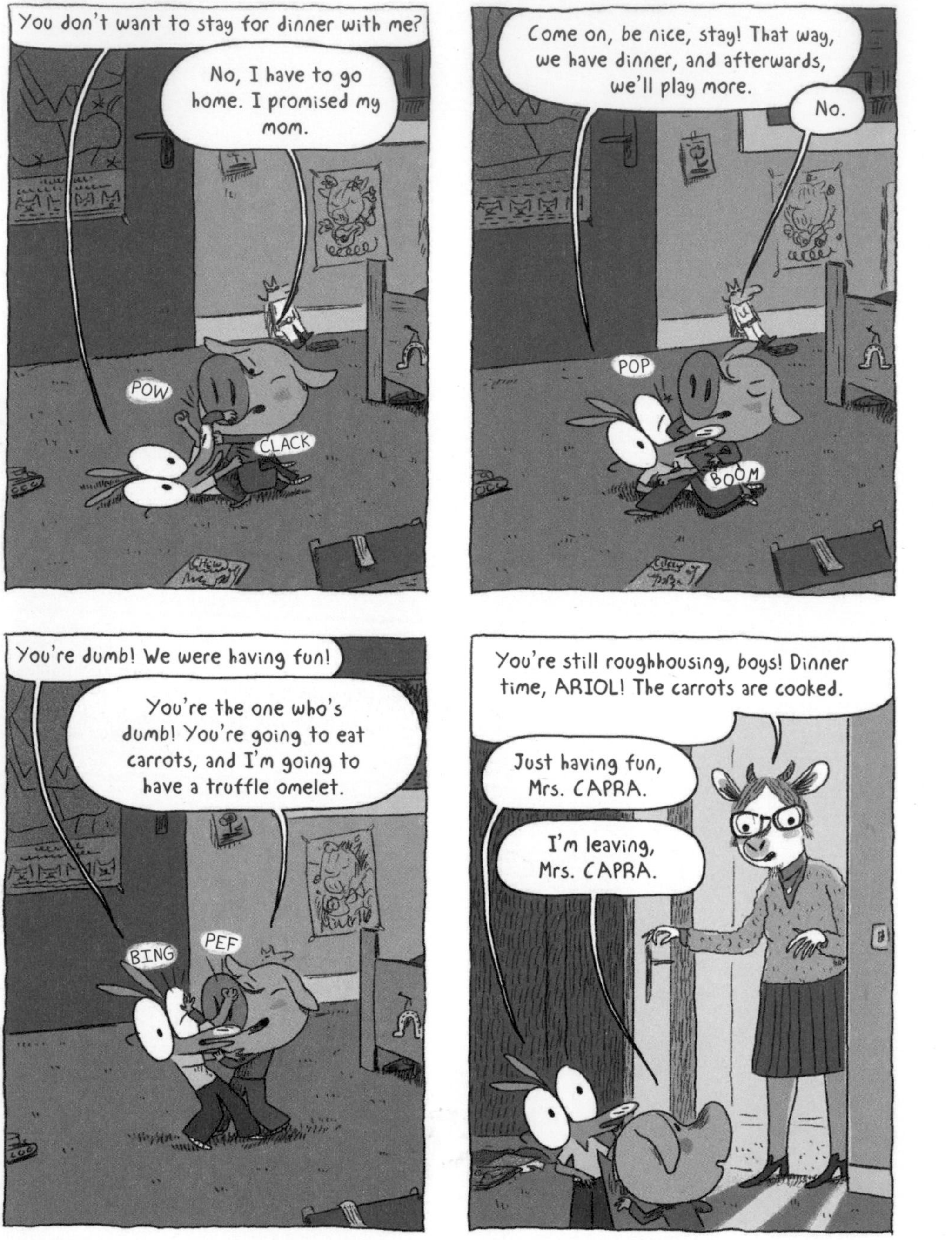
You don't want to stay for dinner with me?
No, I have to go home. I promised my mom.
POW
CLACK
Come on, be nice, stay! That way, we have dinner, and afterwards, we'll play more.
No.
POP
BOOM
You're dumb! We were having fun!
You're the one who's dumb! You're going to eat carrots, and I'm going to have a truffle omelet.
BING
PEF
You're still roughhousing, boys! Dinner time, ARIOL! The carrots are cooked.
Just having fun, Mrs. CAPRA.
I'm leaving, Mrs. CAPRA.

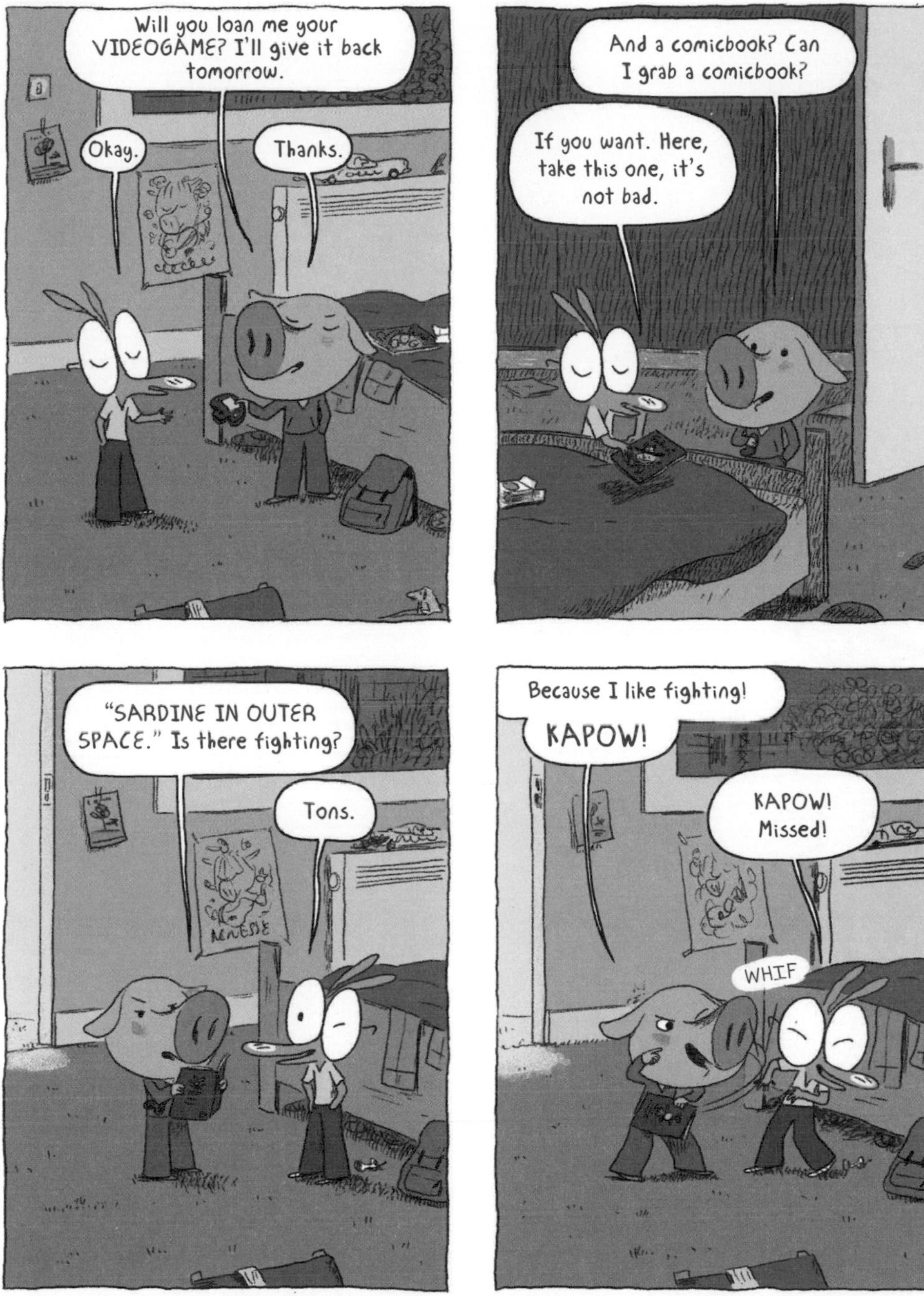
Will you loan me your VIDEOGAME? I'll give it back tomorrow.
Okay.
Thanks.
And a comicbook? Can I grab a comicbook?
If you want. Here, take this one, it's not bad.
"SARDINE IN OUTER SPACE." Is there fighting?
Tons.
Because I like fighting!
KAPOW!
KAPOW! Missed!
WHIF

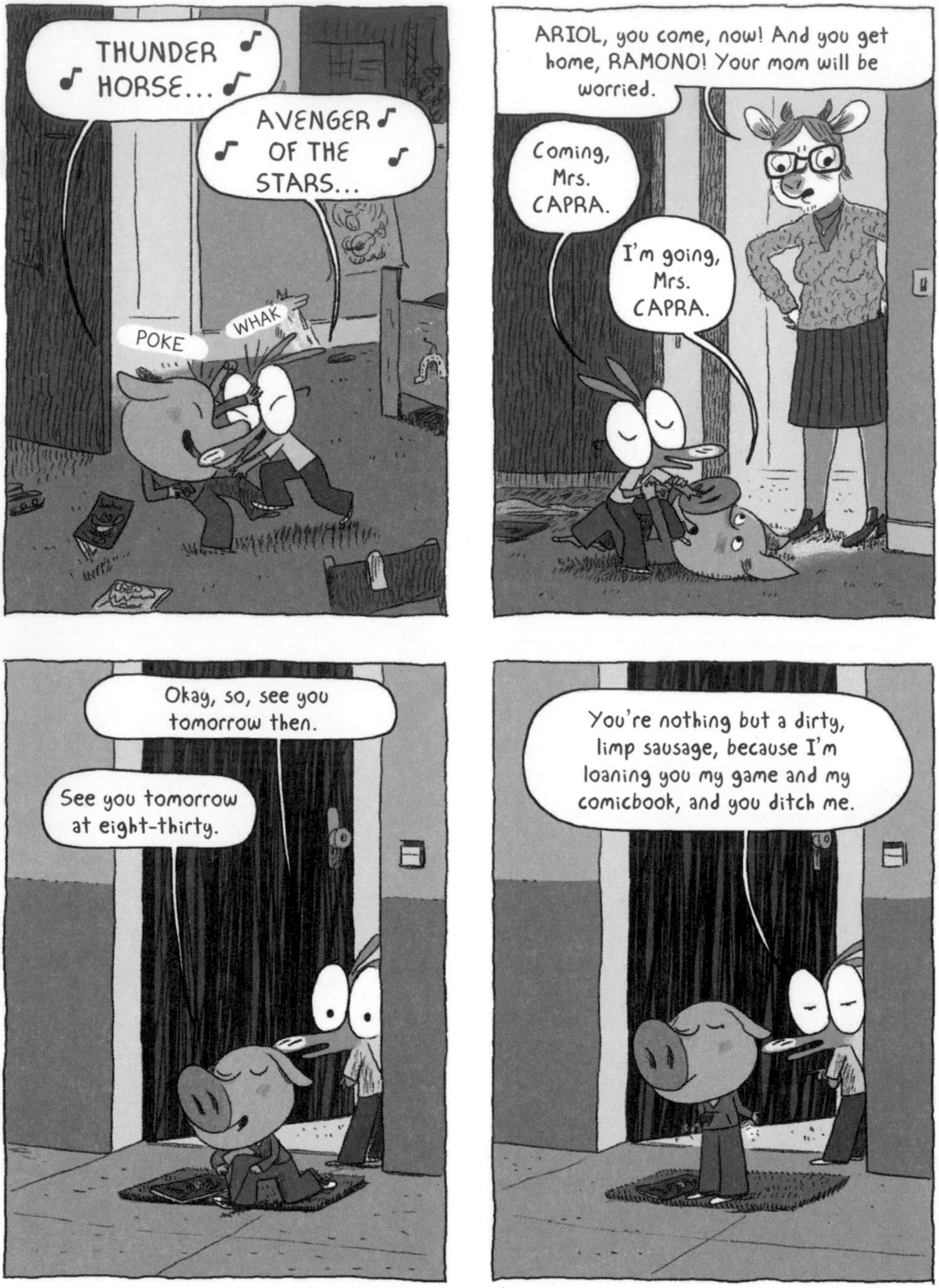
THUNDER HORSE...
AVENGER OF THE STARS...
POKE
WHAK
ARIOL, you come, now! And you get home, RAMONO! Your mom will be worried.
Coming, Mrs. CAPRA.
I'm going, Mrs. CAPRA.
Okay, so, see you tomorrow then.
See you tomorrow at eight-thirty.
You're nothing but a dirty, limp sausage, because I'm loaning you my game and my comicbook, and you ditch me.

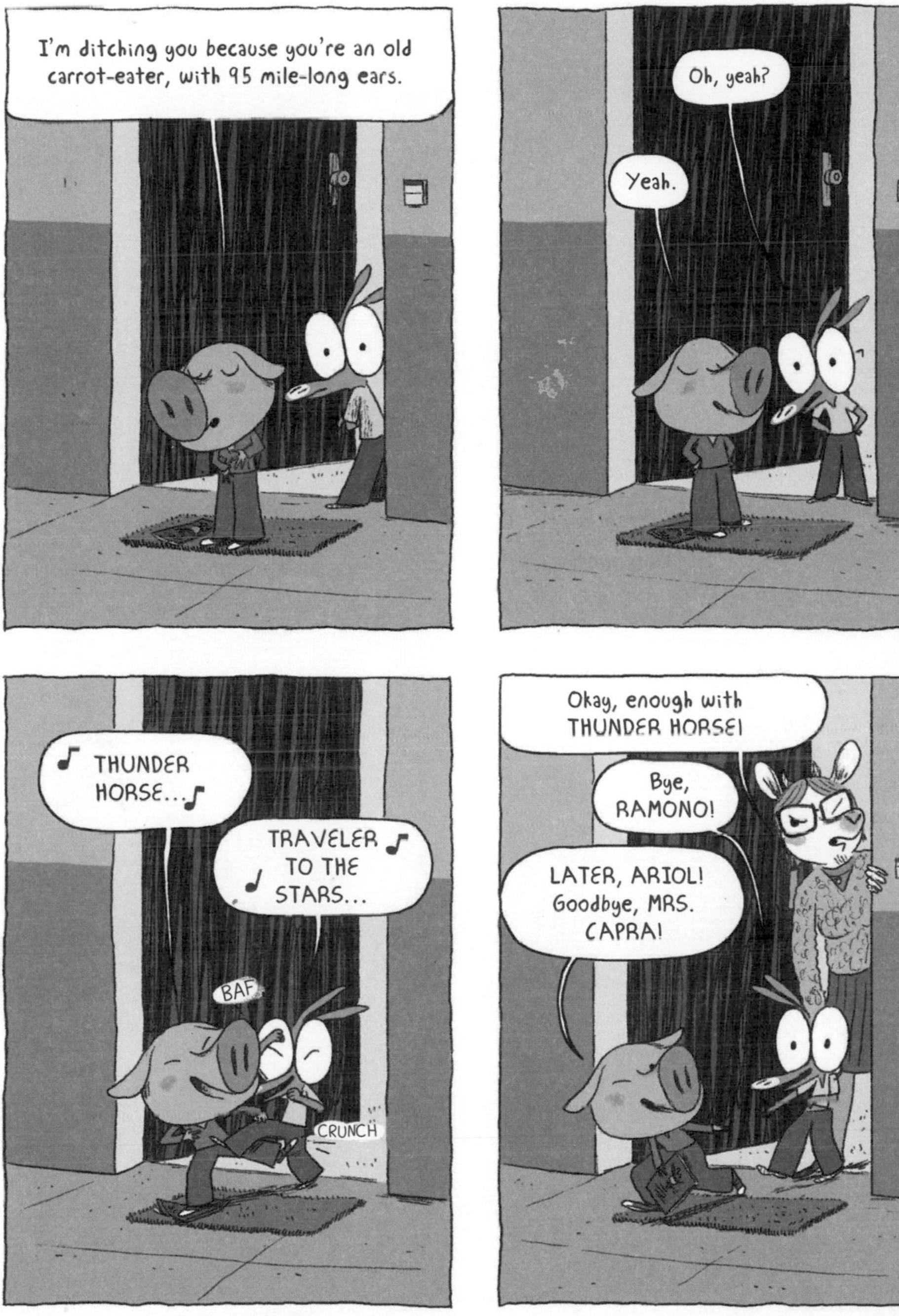
I'm ditching you because you're an old carrot-eater, with 95 mile-long ears.
Oh, yeah?
Yeah.
THUNDER HORSE...
TRAVELER TO THE STARS...
BAF
CRUNCH
Okay, enough with THUNDER HORSE!
Bye, RAMONO!
LATER, ARIOL! Goodbye, MRS. CAPRA!

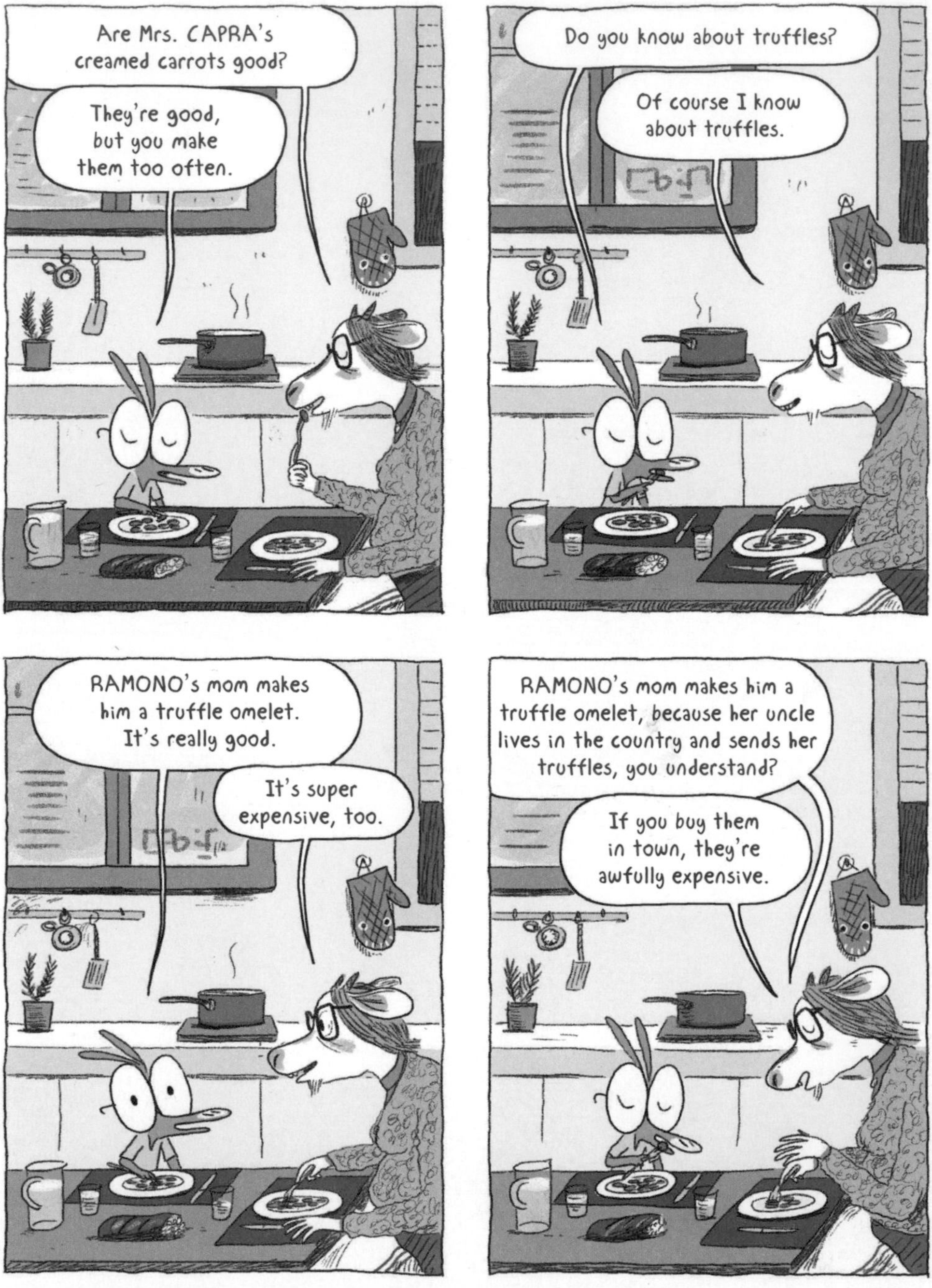

Are Mrs. CAPRA's creamed carrots good?
They're good, but you make them too often.
Do you know about truffles?
Of course I know about truffles.
RAMONO's mom makes him a truffle omelet. It's really good.
It's super expensive, too.
RAMONO's mom makes him a truffle omelet, because her uncle lives in the country and sends her truffles, you understand?
If you buy them in town, they're awfully expensive.

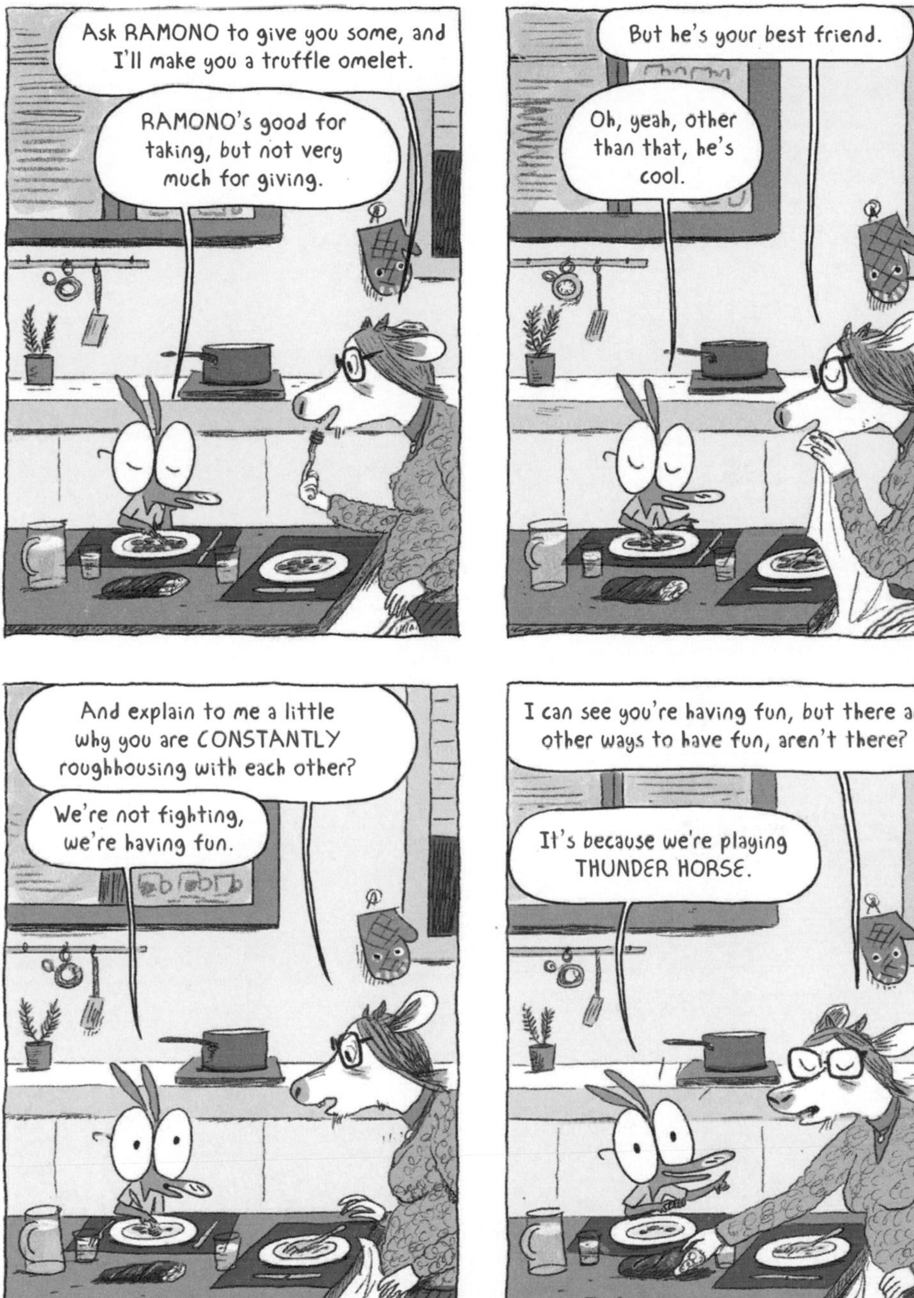
Ask RAMONO to give you some, and I'll make you a truffle omelet.
RAMONO's good for taking, but not very much for giving.
But he's your best friend.
Oh, yeah, other than that, he's cool.
And explain to me a little why you are CONSTANTLY roughhousing with each other?
We're not fighting, we're having fun.
I can see you're having fun, but there are other ways to have fun, aren't there?
It's because we're playing THUNDER HORSE.

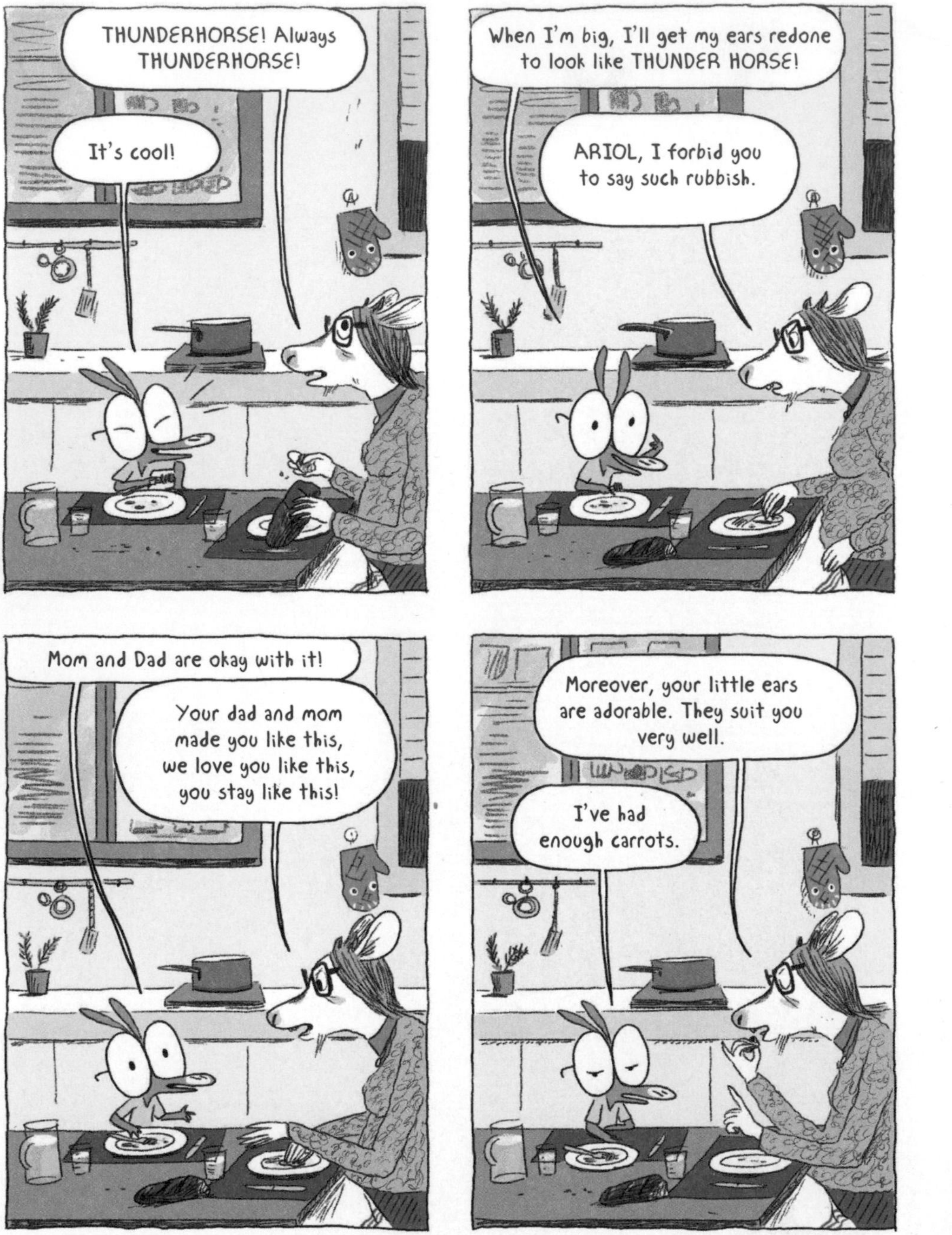
THUNDERHORSE! Always THUNDERHORSE!
It's cool!
When I'm big, I'll get my ears redone to look like THUNDER HORSE!
ARIOL, I forbid you to say such rubbish.
Mom and Dad are okay with it!
Your dad and mom made you like this, we love you like this, you stay like this!
Moreover, your little ears are adorable. They suit you very well.
I've had enough carrots.

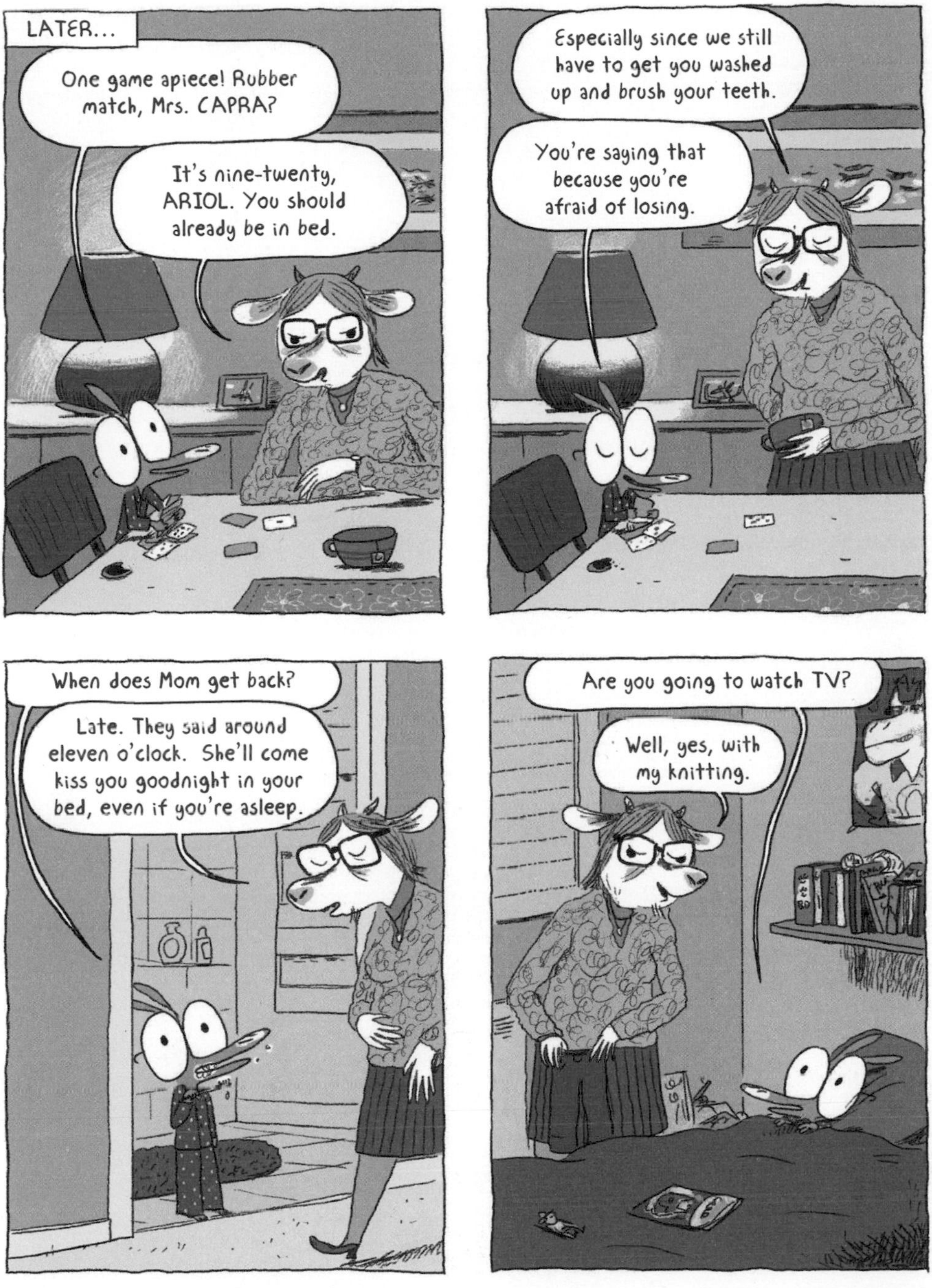
LATER...
One game apiece! Rubber match, Mrs. CAPRA?
It's nine-twenty, ARIOL. You should already be in bed.
Especially since we still have to get you washed up and brush your teeth.
You're saying that because you're afraid of losing.
When does Mom get back?
Late. They said around eleven o'clock. She'll come kiss you goodnight in your bed, even if you're asleep.
Are you going to watch TV?
Well, yes, with my knitting.

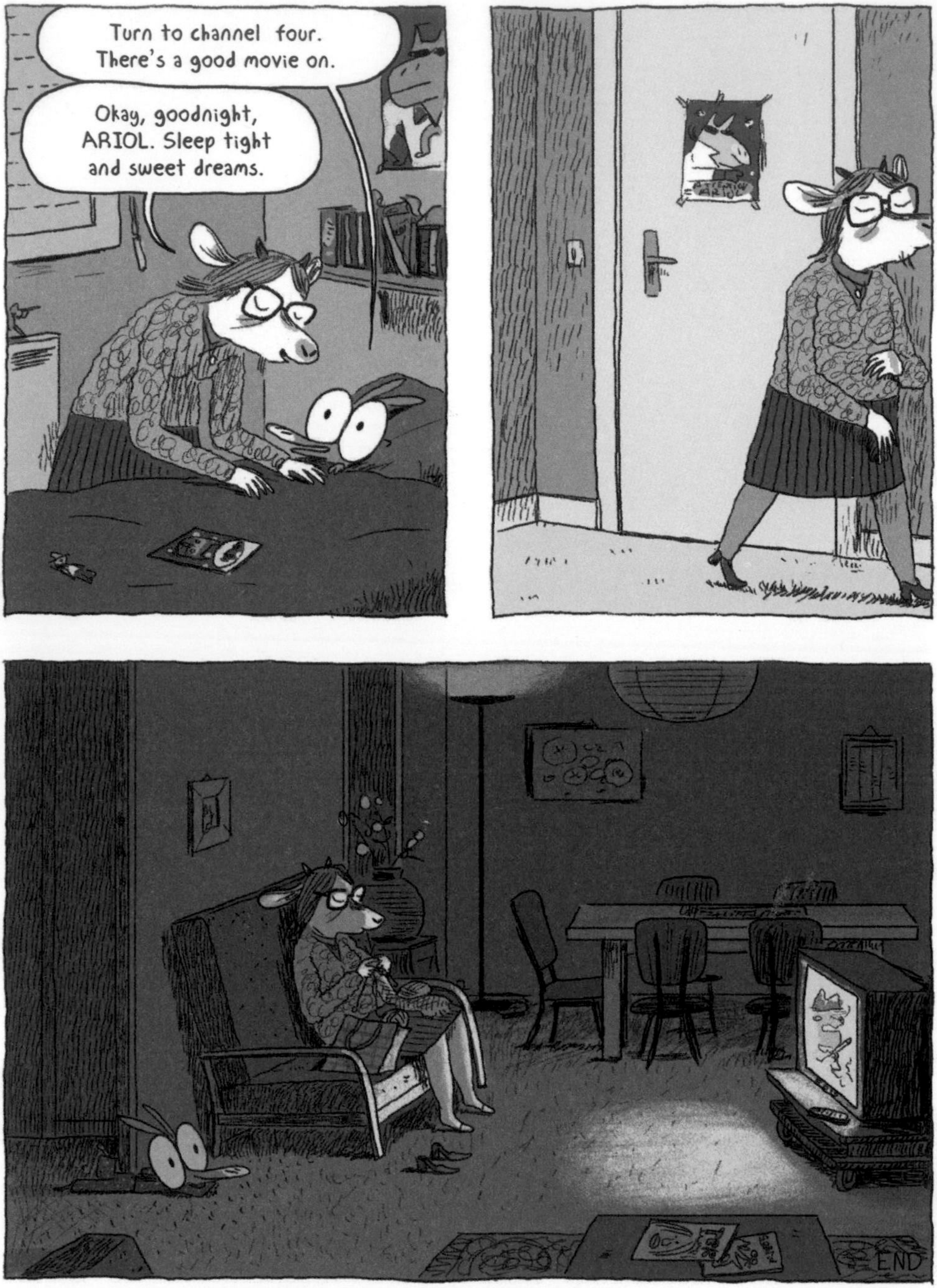
Turn to channel four. There's a good movie on.
Okay, goodnight, ARIOL. Sleep tight and sweet dreams.
END

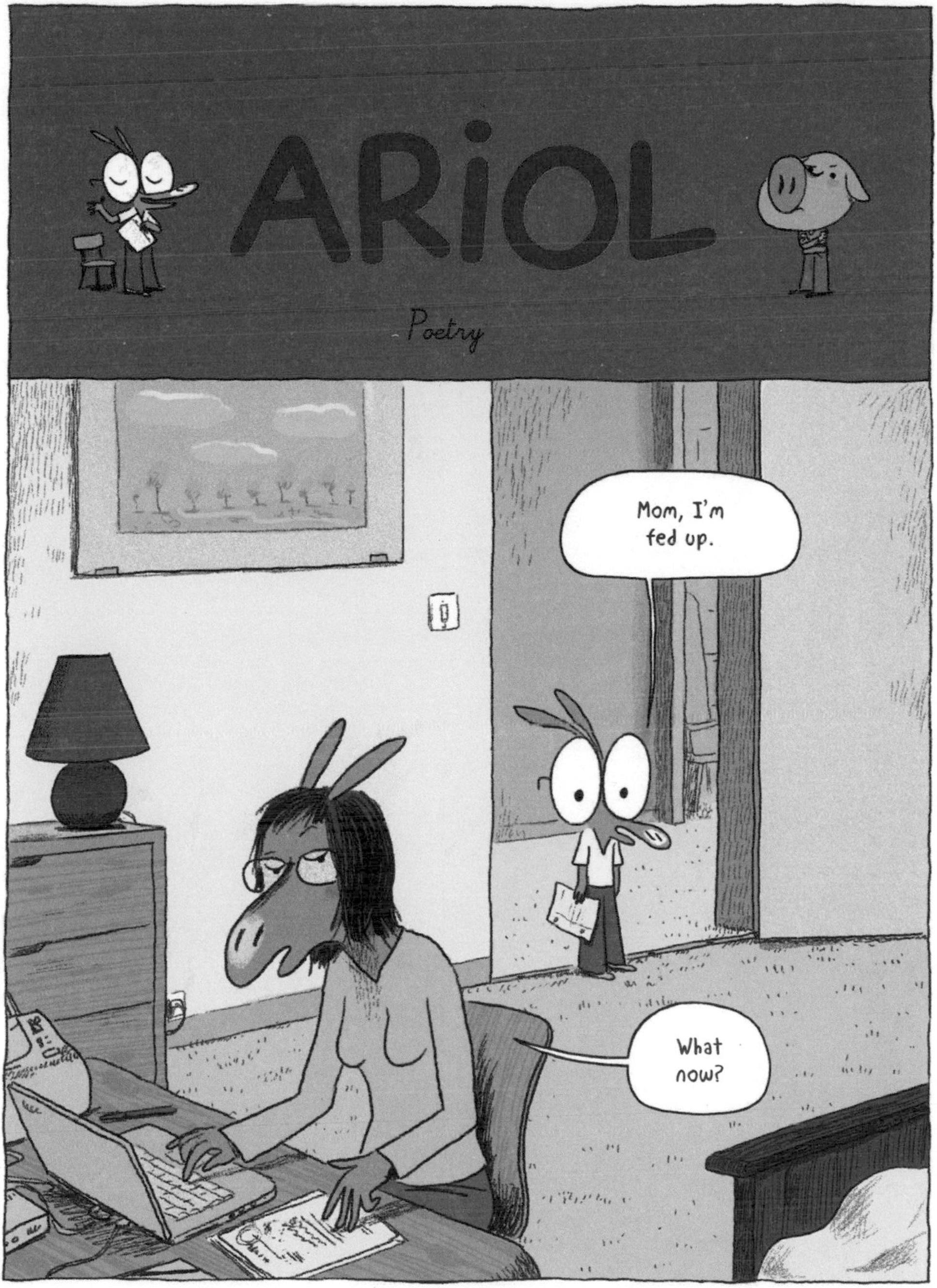
ARiOL
Poetry
Mom, I'm fed up.
What now?

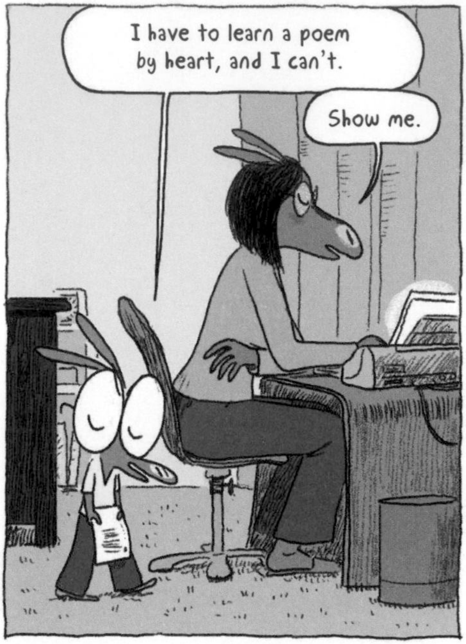
I have to learn a poem by heart, and I can't.
Show me.

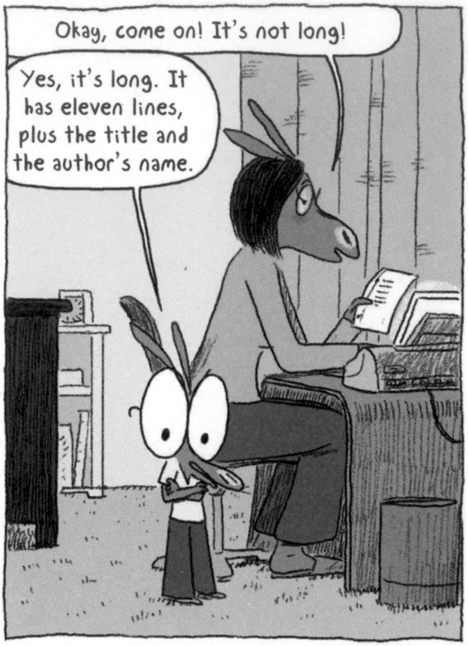
Okay, come on! It's not long!
Yes, it's long. It has eleven lines, plus the title and the author's name.

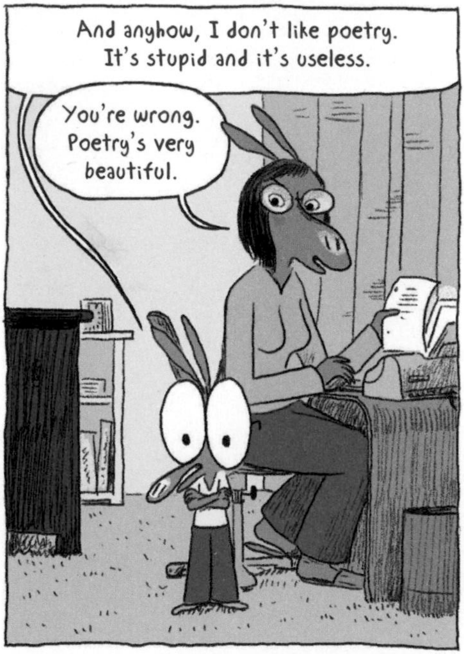
And anyhow, I don't like poetry. It's stupid and it's useless.
You're wrong. Poetry's very beautiful.

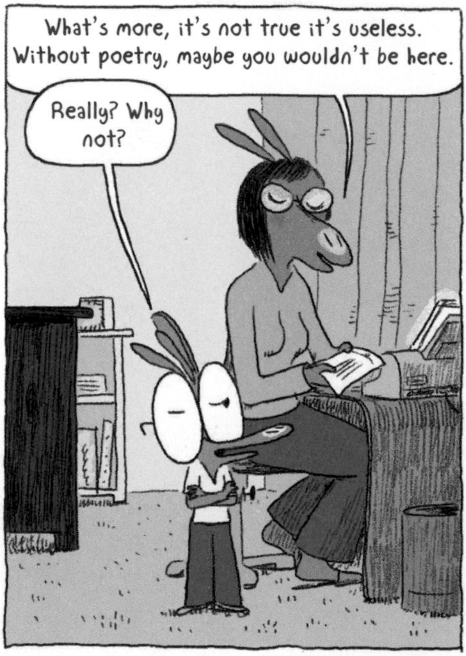
What's more, it's not true it's useless. Without poetry, maybe you wouldn't be here.
Really? Why not?

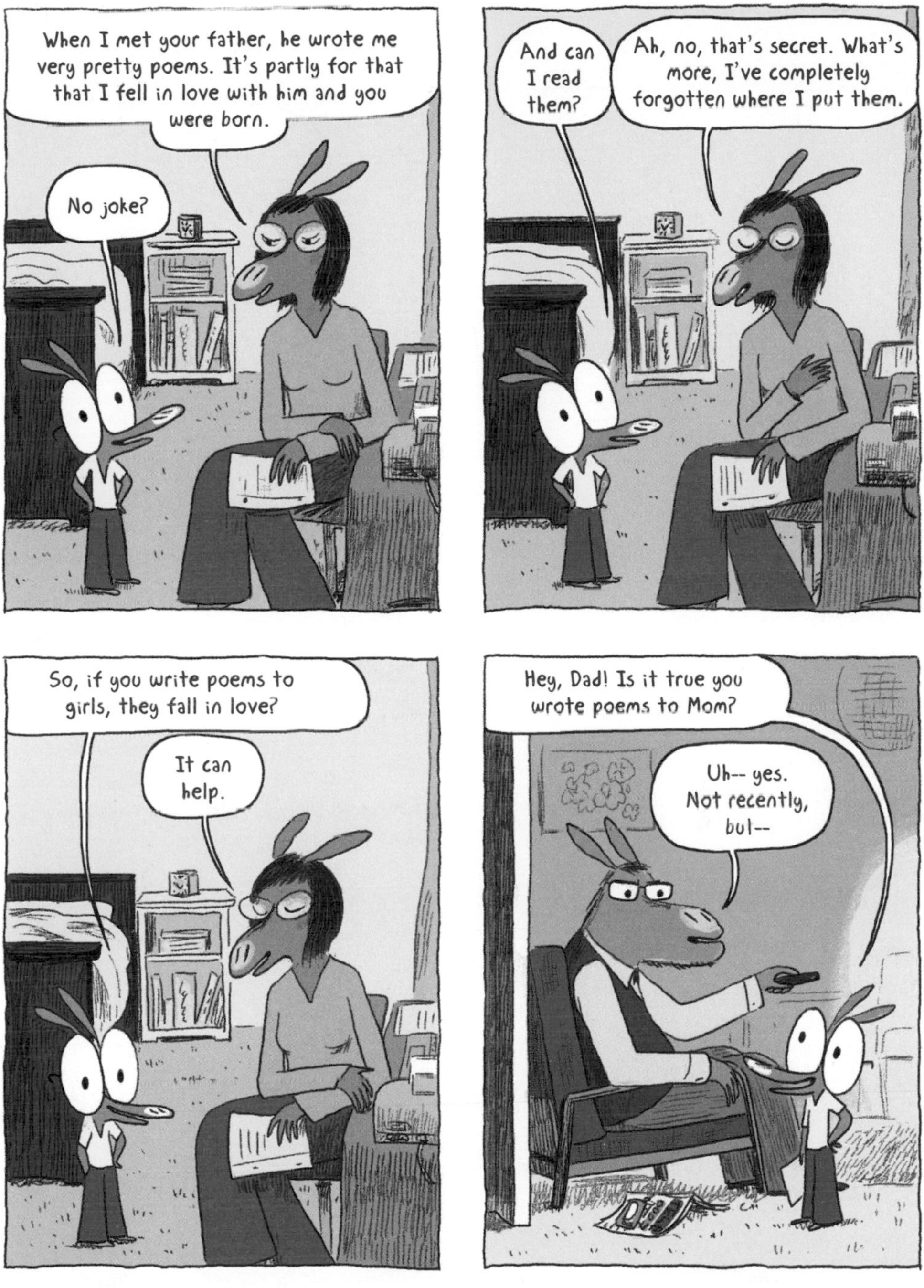
When I met your father, he wrote me very pretty poems. It's partly for that that I fell in love with him and you were born.
No joke?
And can I read them?
Ah, no, that's secret. What's more, I've completely forgotten where I put them.
So, if you write poems to girls, they fall in love?
It can help.
Hey, Dad! Is it true you wrote poems to Mom?
Uh-- yes. Not recently, but--

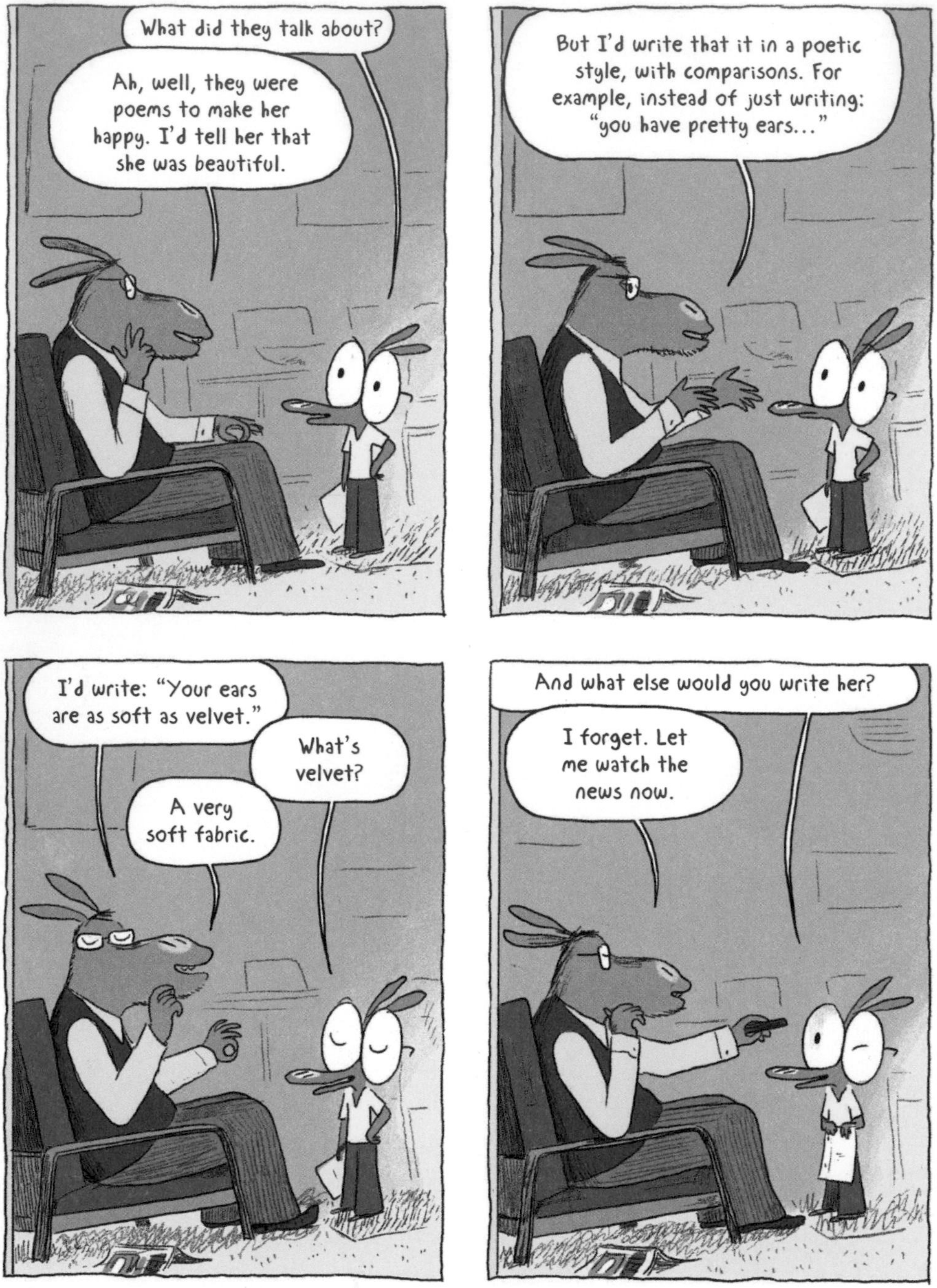
What did they talk about?
Ah, well, they were poems to make her happy. I'd tell her that she was beautiful.
But I'd write that it in a poetic style, with comparisons. For example, instead of just writing: "you have pretty ears..."
I'd write: "Your ears are as soft as velvet."
What's velvet?
A very soft fabric.
And what else would you write her?
I forget. Let me watch the news now.

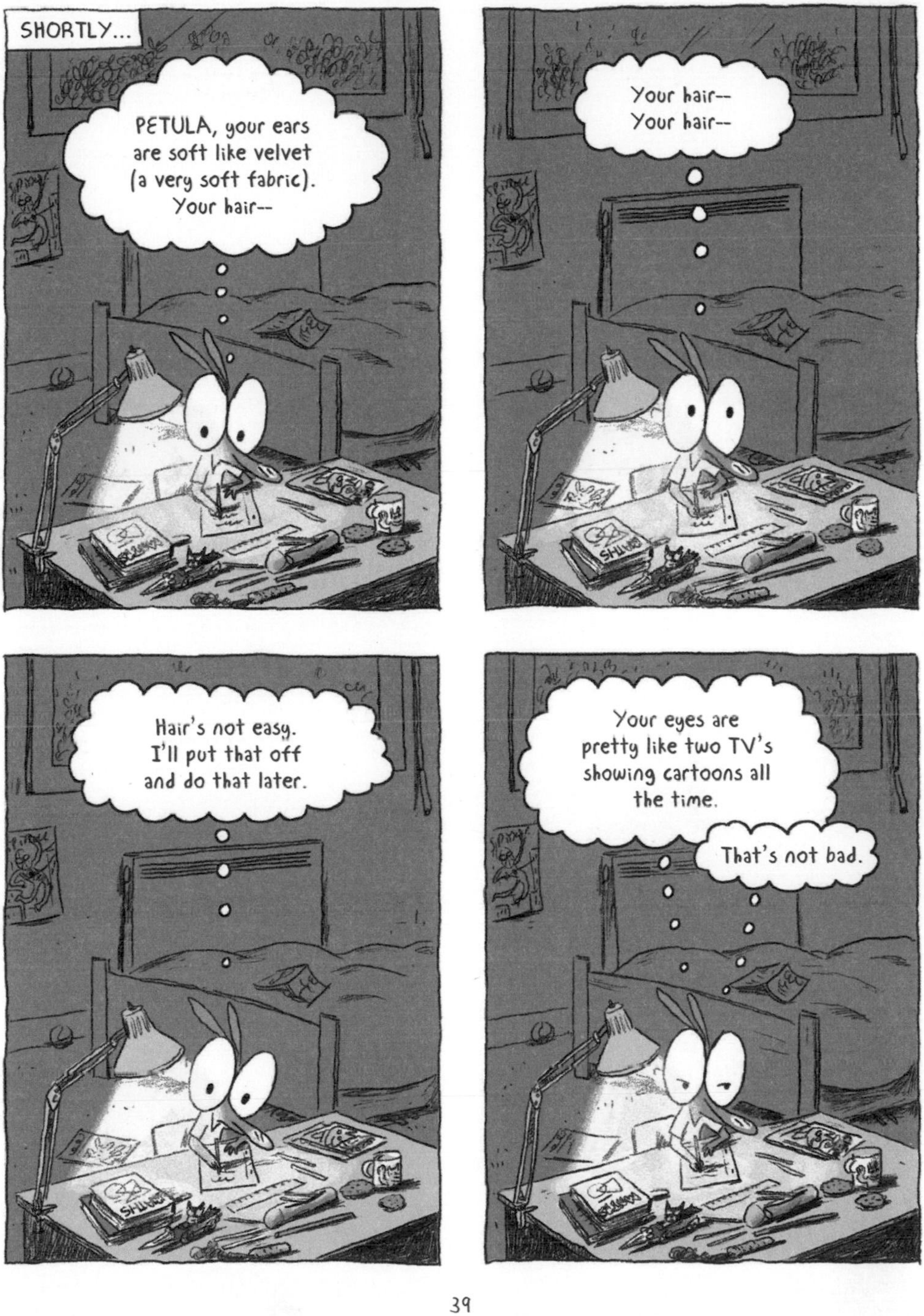
SHORTLY...
PETULA, your ears are soft like velvet (a very soft fabric). Your hair--
Your hair-- Your hair--
Hair's not easy. I'll put that off and do that later.
Your eyes are pretty like two TV's showing cartoons all the time.
That's not bad.

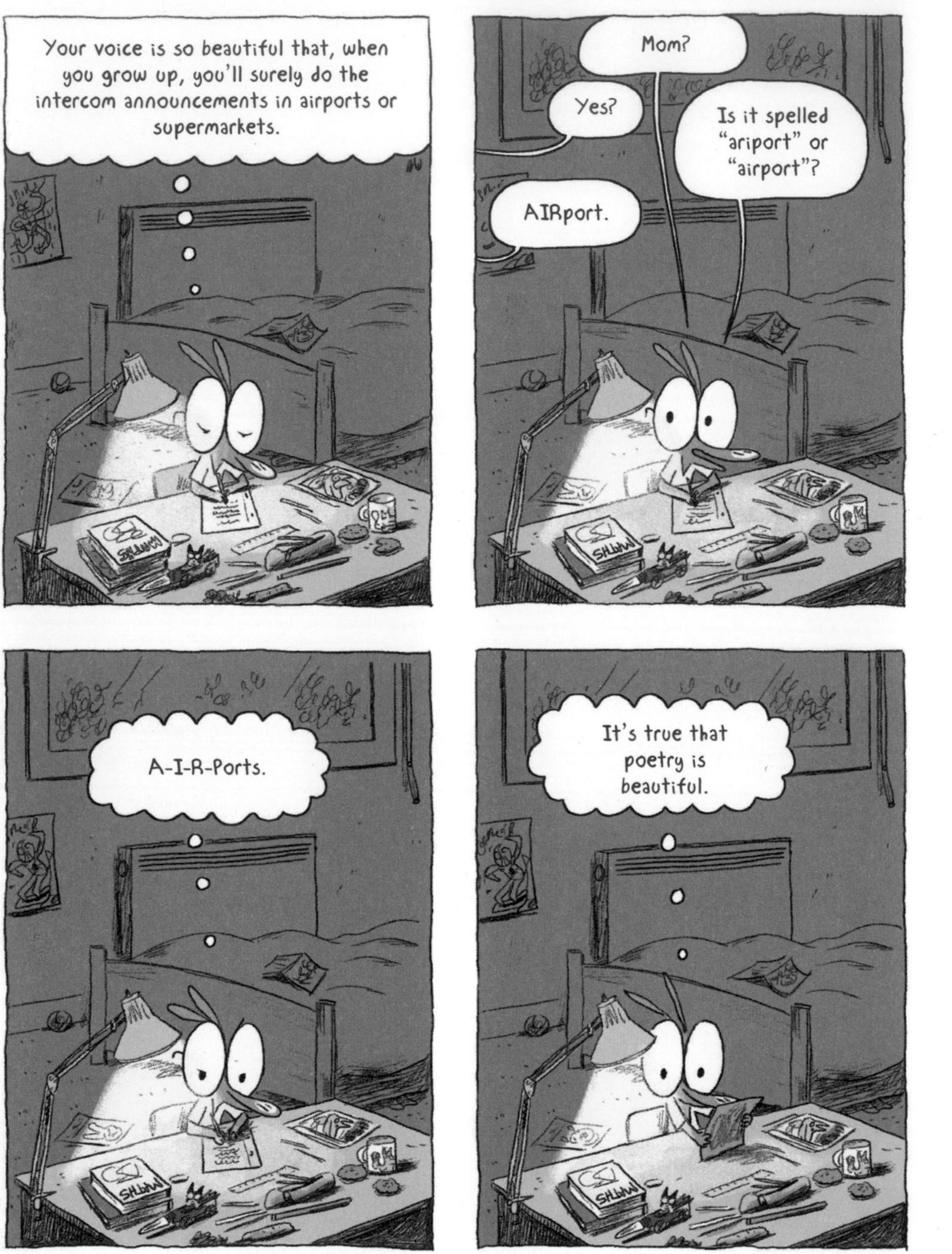
Your voice is so beautiful that, when you grow up, you'll surely do the intercom announcements in airports or supermarkets.
Mom?
Yes?
Is it spelled "ariport" or "airport"?
AIRport.
A-I-R-Ports.
It's true that poetry is beautiful.

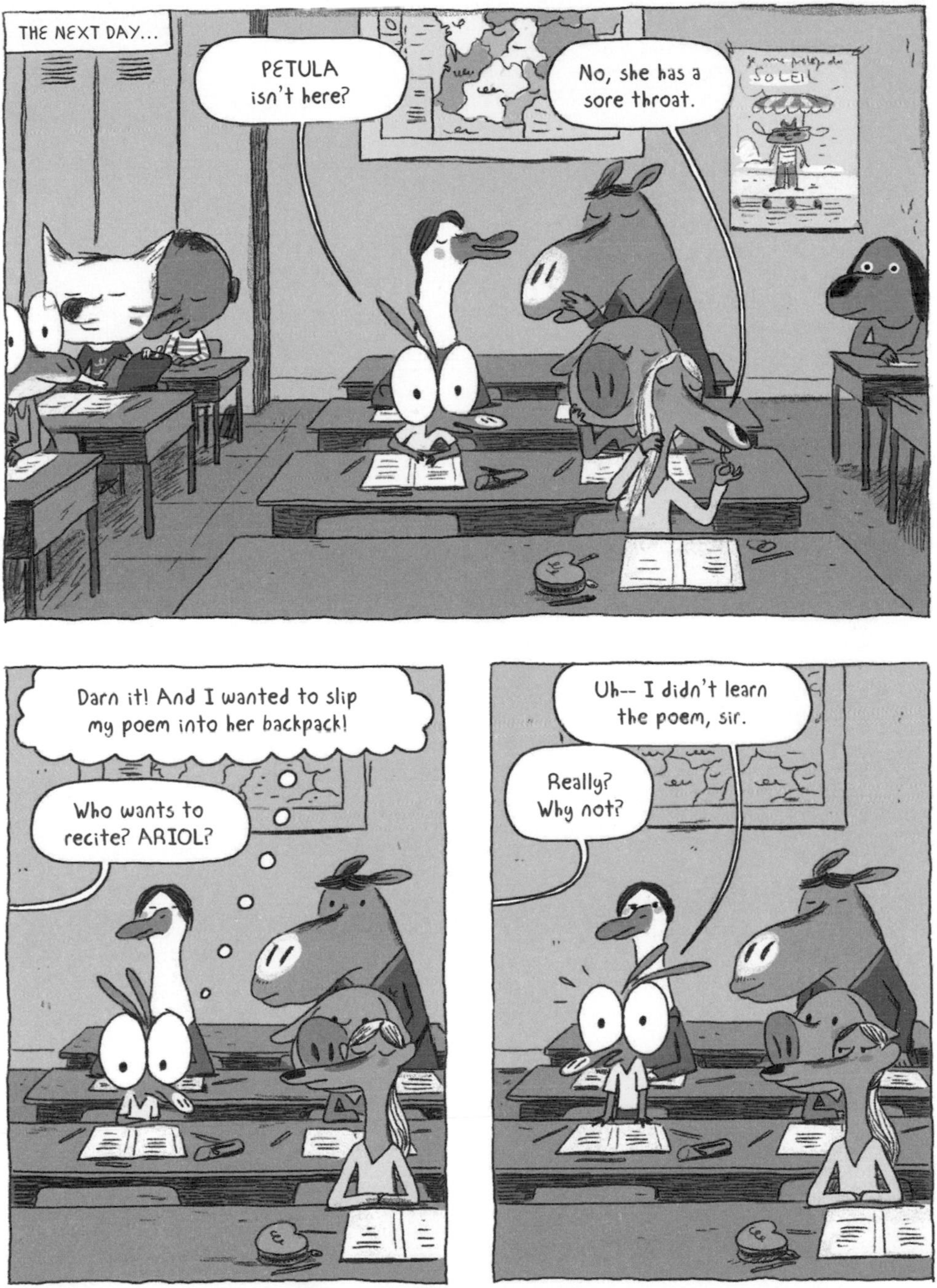
THE NEXT DAY...
PETULA isn't here?
No, she has a sore throat.
Darn it! And I wanted to slip my poem into her backpack!
Who wants to recite? ARIOL?
Uh-- I didn't learn the poem, sir.
Really? Why not?

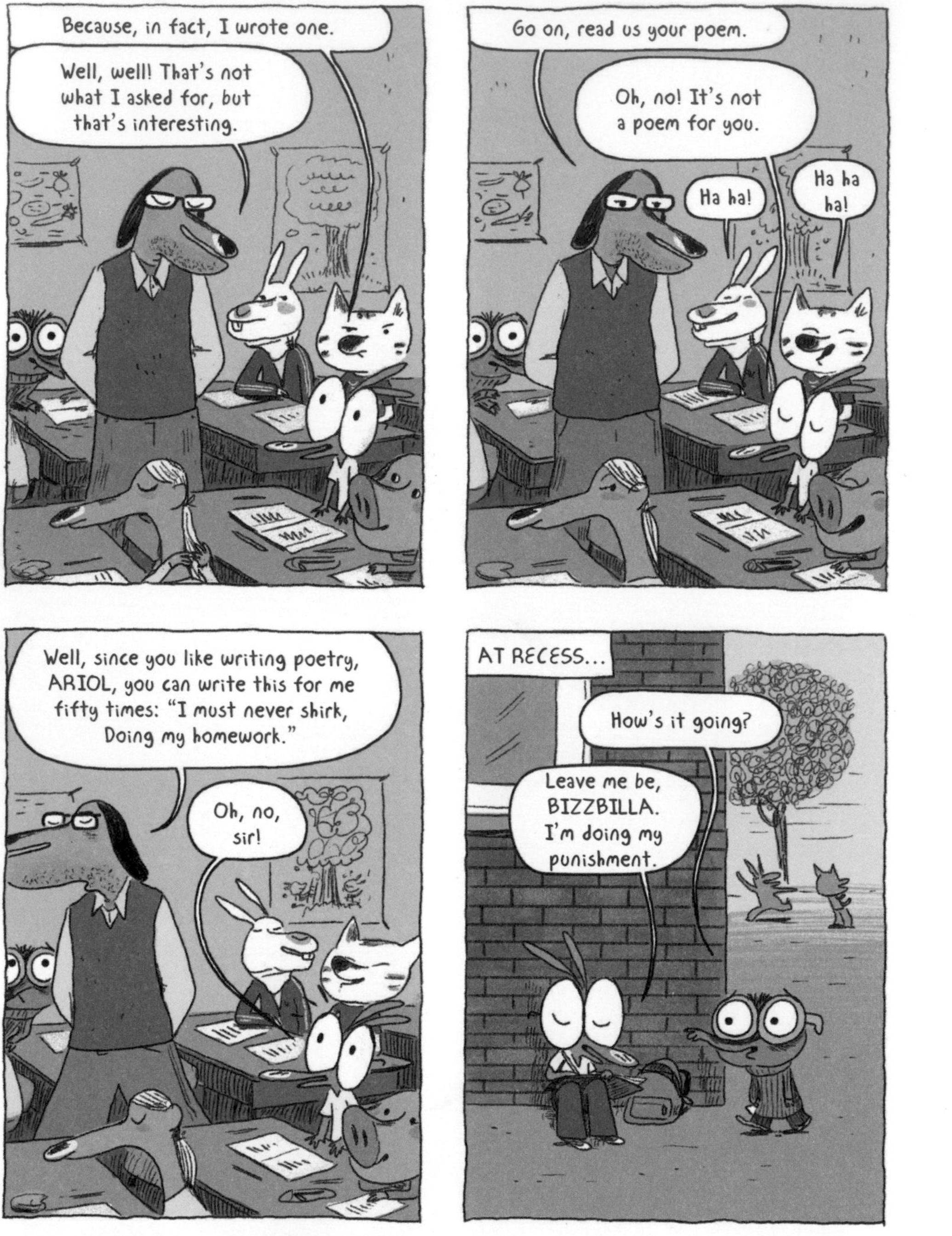
Because, in fact, I wrote one.
Well, well! That's not what I asked for, but that's interesting.
Go on, read us your poem.
Oh, no! It's not a poem for you.
Ha ha!
Ha ha ha!
Well, since you like writing poetry, ARIOL, you can write this for me fifty times: "I must never shirk, Doing my homework."
Oh, no, sir!
AT RECESS...
How's it going?
Leave me be, BIZZBILLA. I'm doing my punishment.

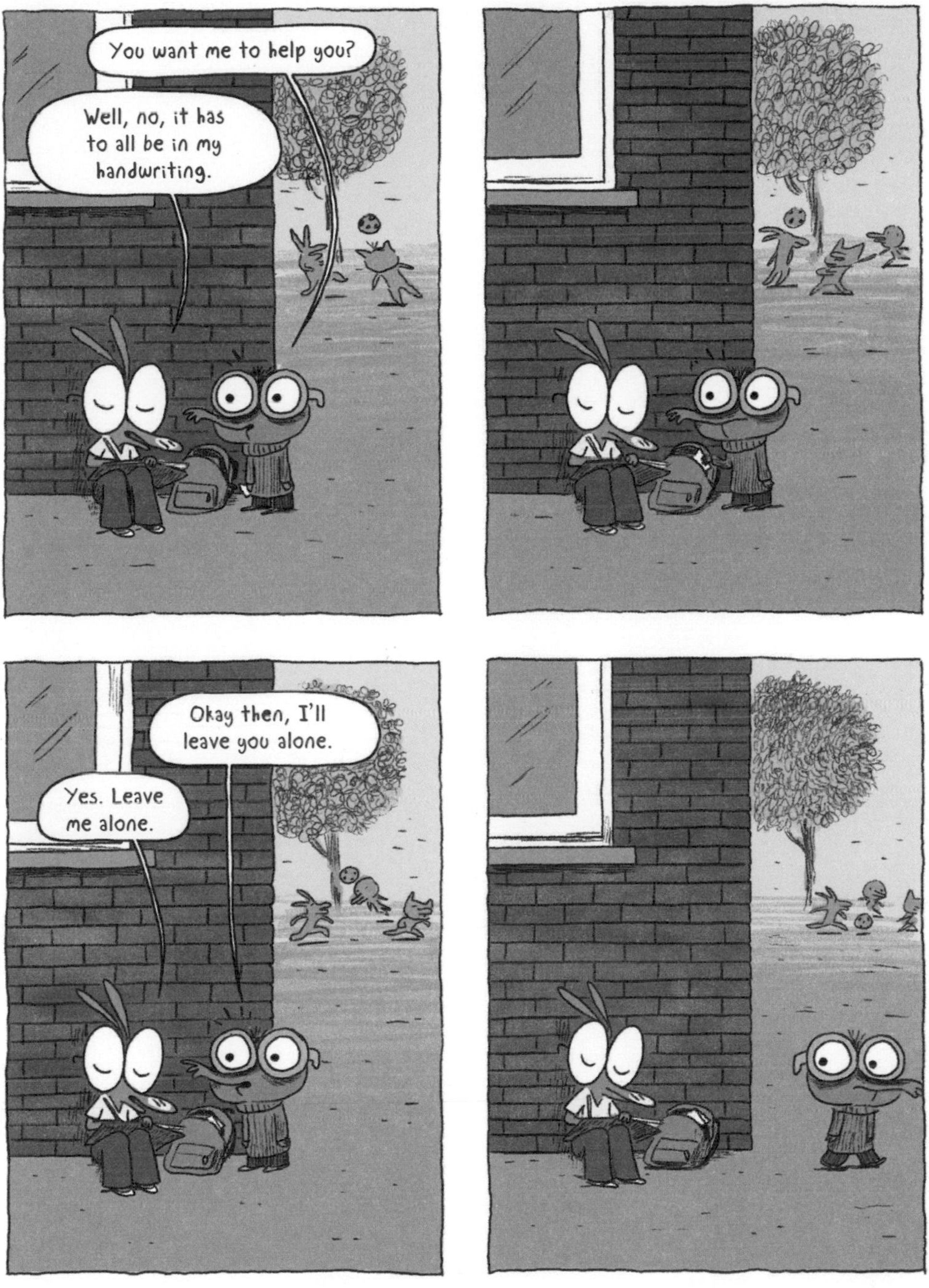
You want me to help you?
Well, no, it has to all be in my handwriting.
Okay then, I'll leave you alone.
Yes. Leave me alone.

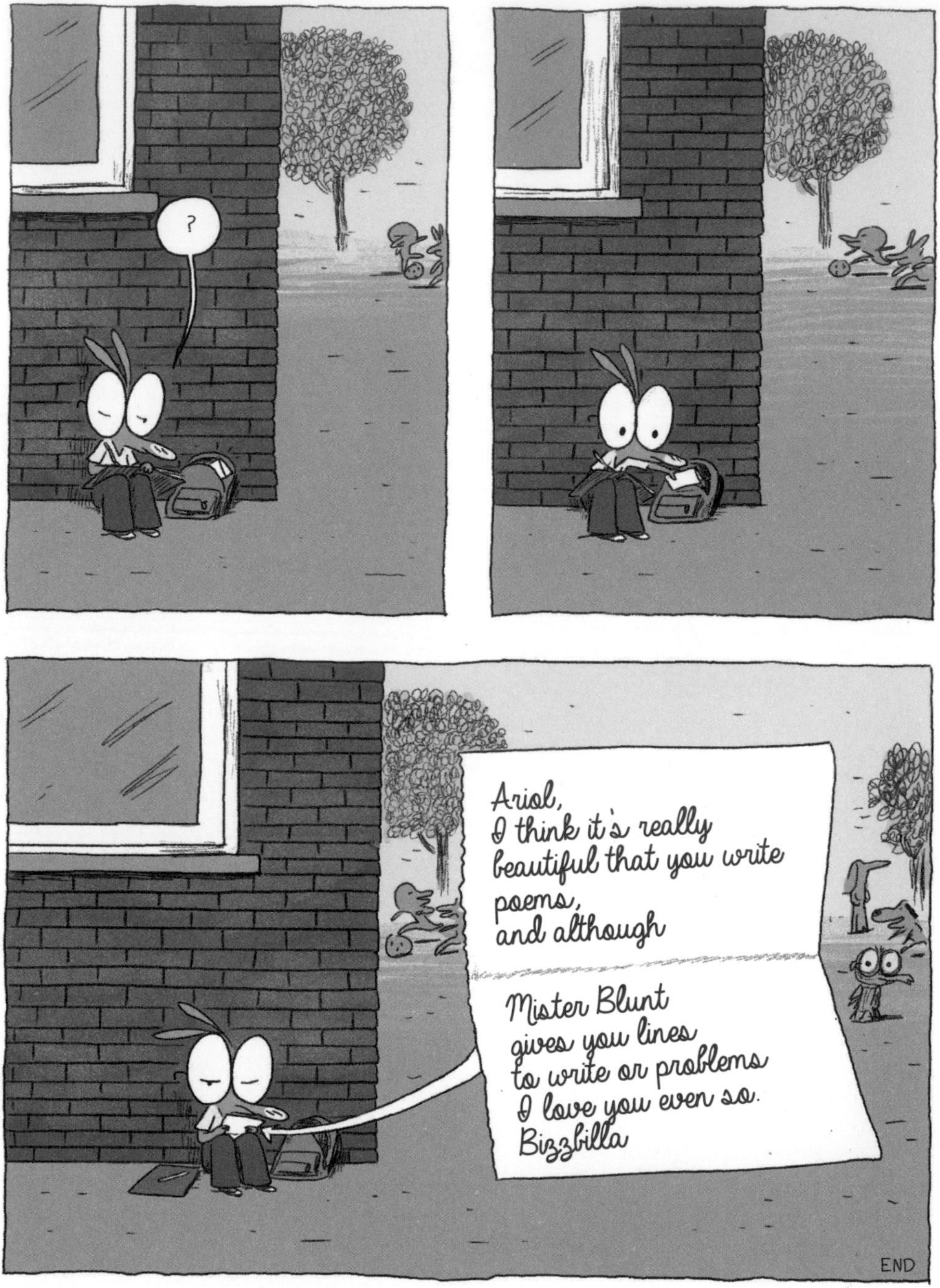
?
Ariol,
I think it's really
beautiful that you write
poems,
and although
Mister Blunt
gives you lines
to write or problems
I love you even so.
Bizzbilla
END

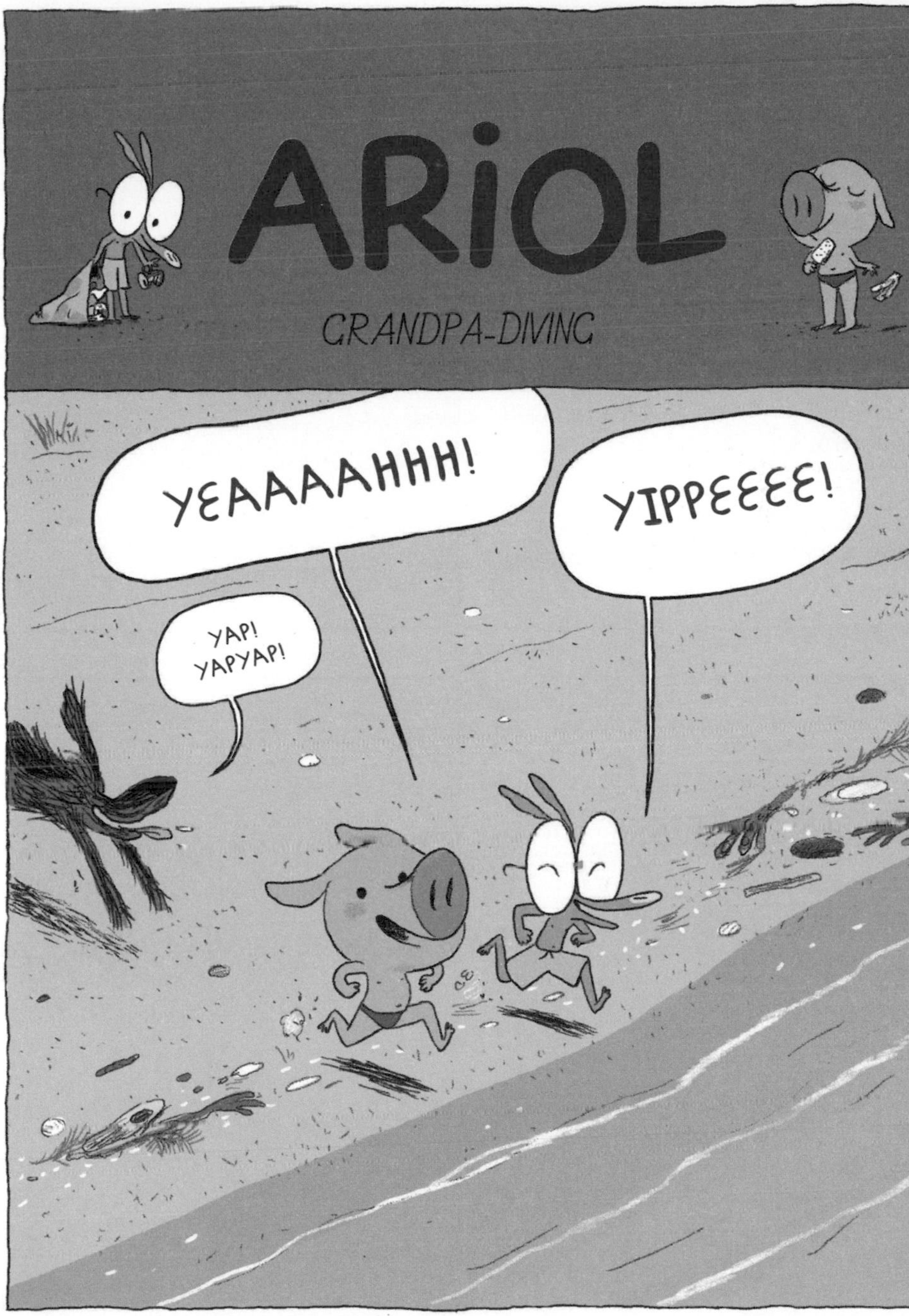
ARiOL
GRANDPA-DIVING
YAP! YAPYAP!
YEAAAAAHHH!
YIPPEEEE!

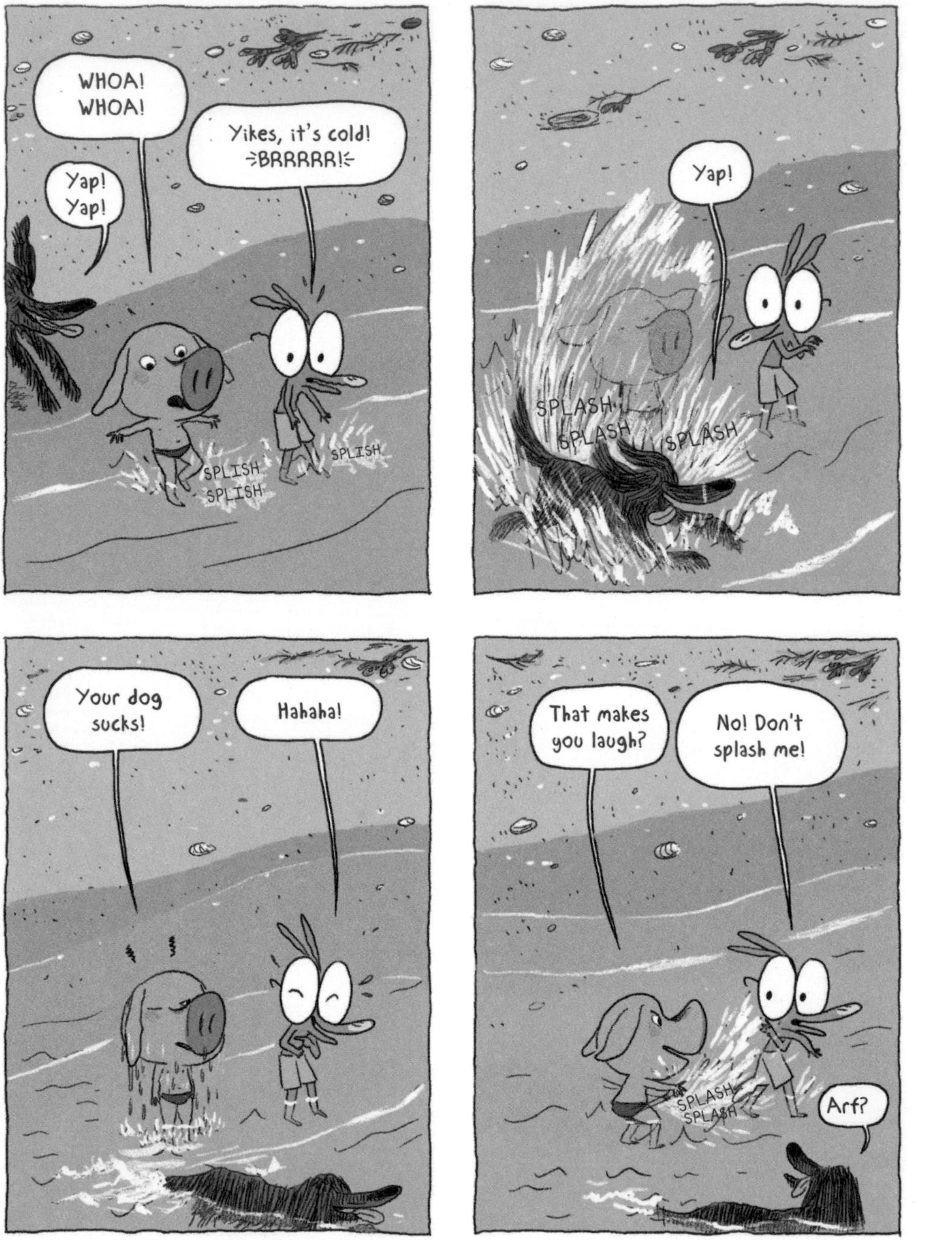
WHOA! WHOA!
Yap! Yap!
Yikes, it's cold! BRRRRR!
SPLISH SPLISH
SPLISH
Yap!
SPLASH
SPLASH
SPLASH
Your dog sucks!
Hahaha!
That makes you laugh?
No! Don't splash me!
SPLASH SPLASH
Arf?

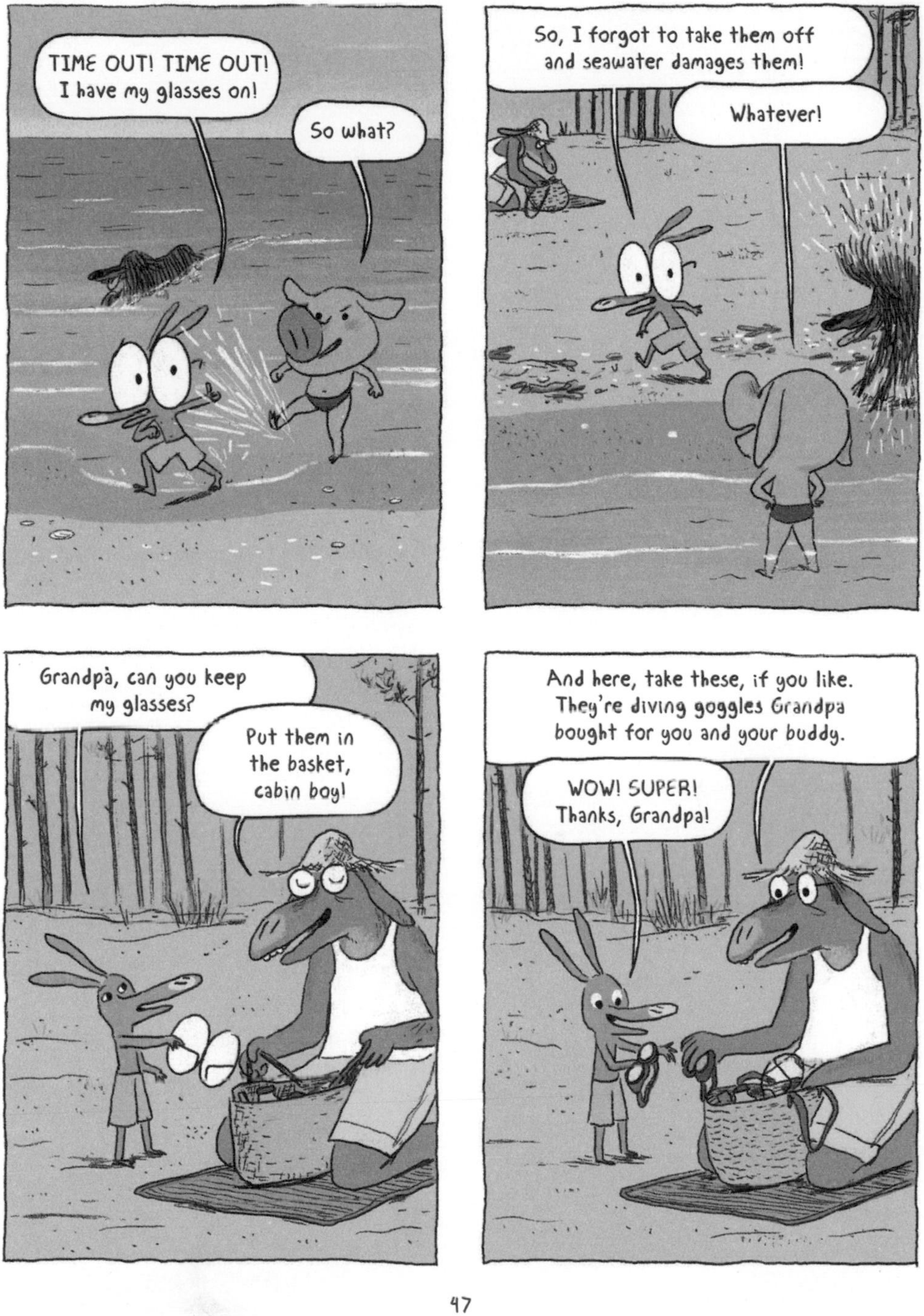
TIME OUT! TIME OUT! I have my glasses on!
So what?
So, I forgot to take them off and seawater damages them!
Whatever!
Grandpà, can you keep my glasses?
Put them in the basket, cabin boy!
And here, take these, if you like. They're diving goggles Grandpa bought for you and your buddy.
WOW! SUPER! Thanks, Grandpa!

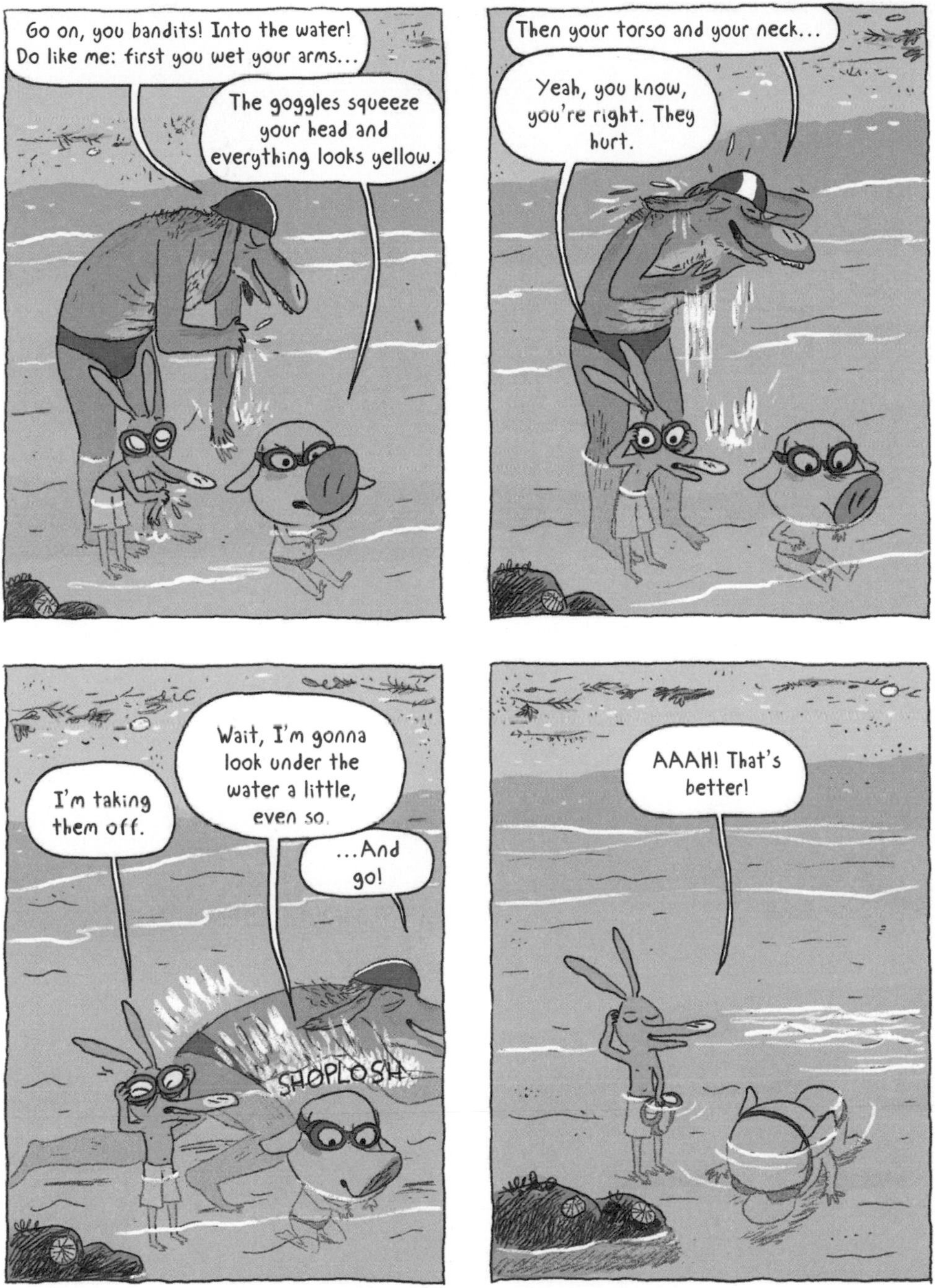
Go on, you bandits! Into the water! Do like me: first you wet your arms...
The goggles squeeze your head and everything looks yellow.
Then your torso and your neck...
Yeah, you know, you're right. They hurt.
I'm taking them off.
Wait, I'm gonna look under the water a little, even so.
...And go!
SHOPLOSH
AAAH! That's better!

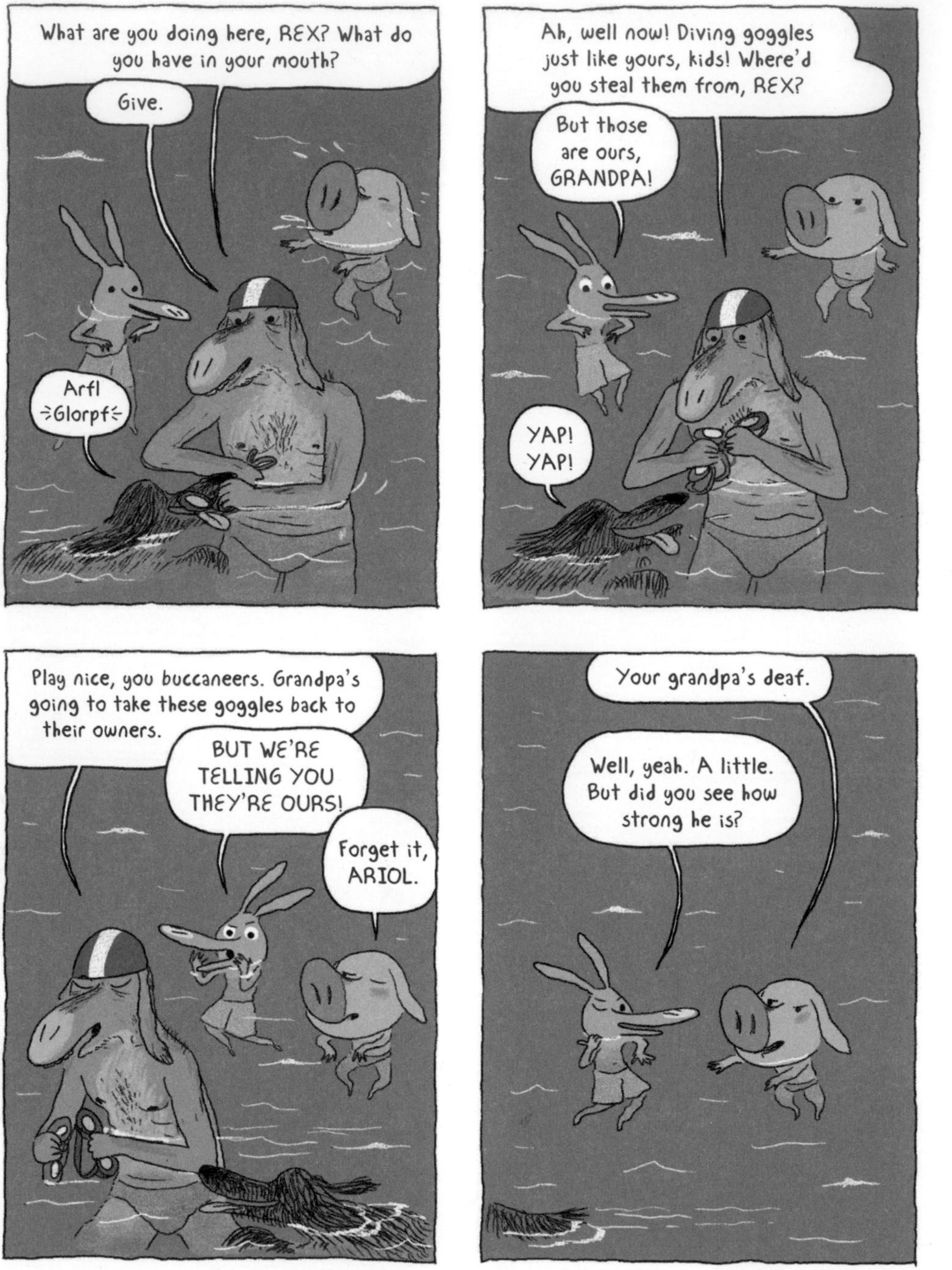
What are you doing here, REX? What do you have in your mouth?
Give.
Arfl
Glorpf
Ah, well now! Diving goggles just like yours, kids! Where'd you steal them from, REX?
But those are ours, GRANDPA!
YAP! YAP!
Play nice, you buccaneers. Grandpa's going to take these goggles back to their owners.
BUT WE'RE TELLING YOU THEY'RE OURS!
Forget it, ARIOL.
Your grandpa's deaf.
Well, yeah. A little. But did you see how strong he is?

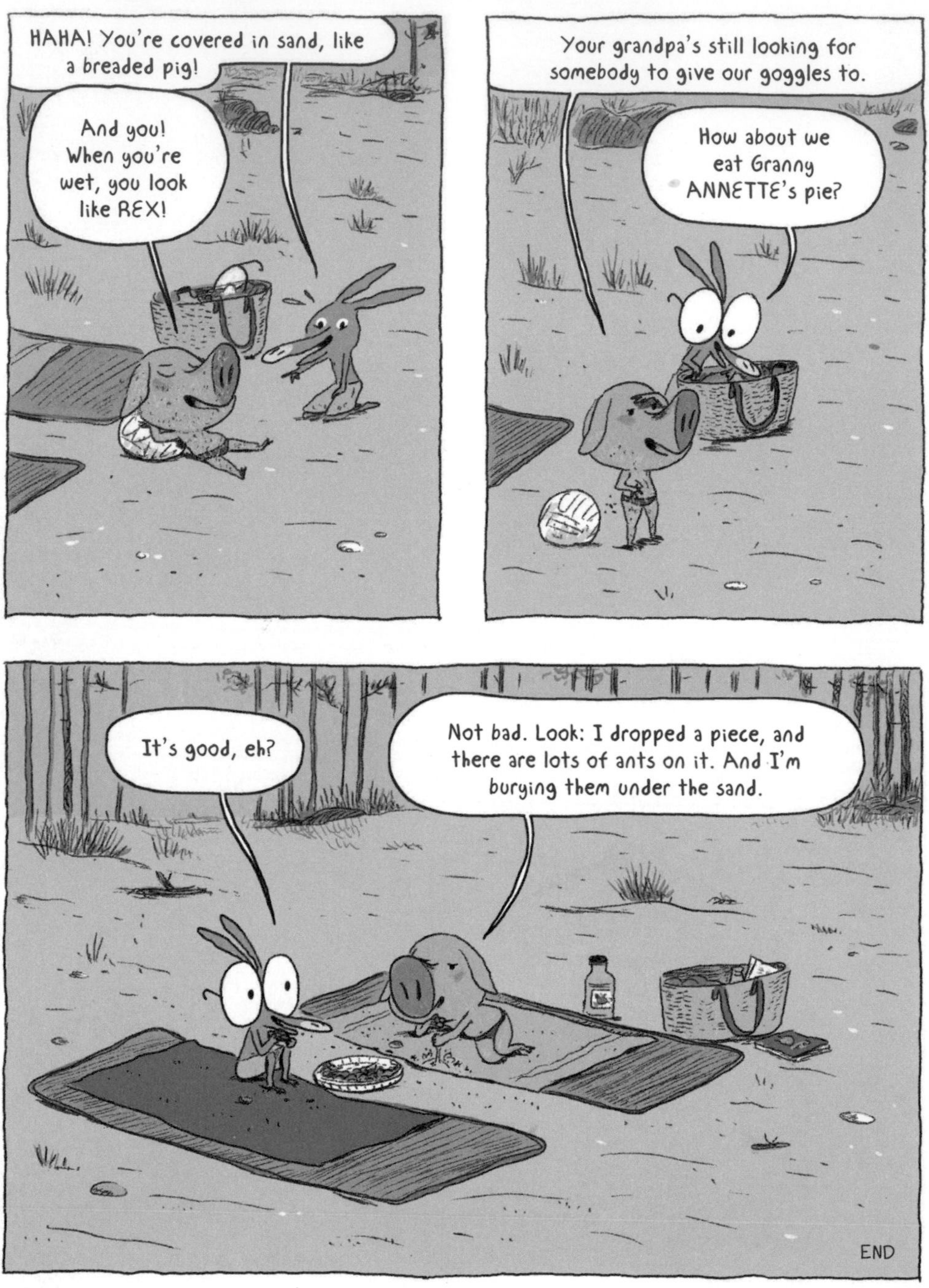
HAHA! You're covered in sand, like a breaded pig!
And you! When you're wet, you look like REX!
Your grandpa's still looking for somebody to give our goggles to.
How about we eat Granny ANNETTE's pie?
It's good, eh?
Not bad. Look: I dropped a piece, and there are lots of ants on it. And I'm burying them under the sand.
END

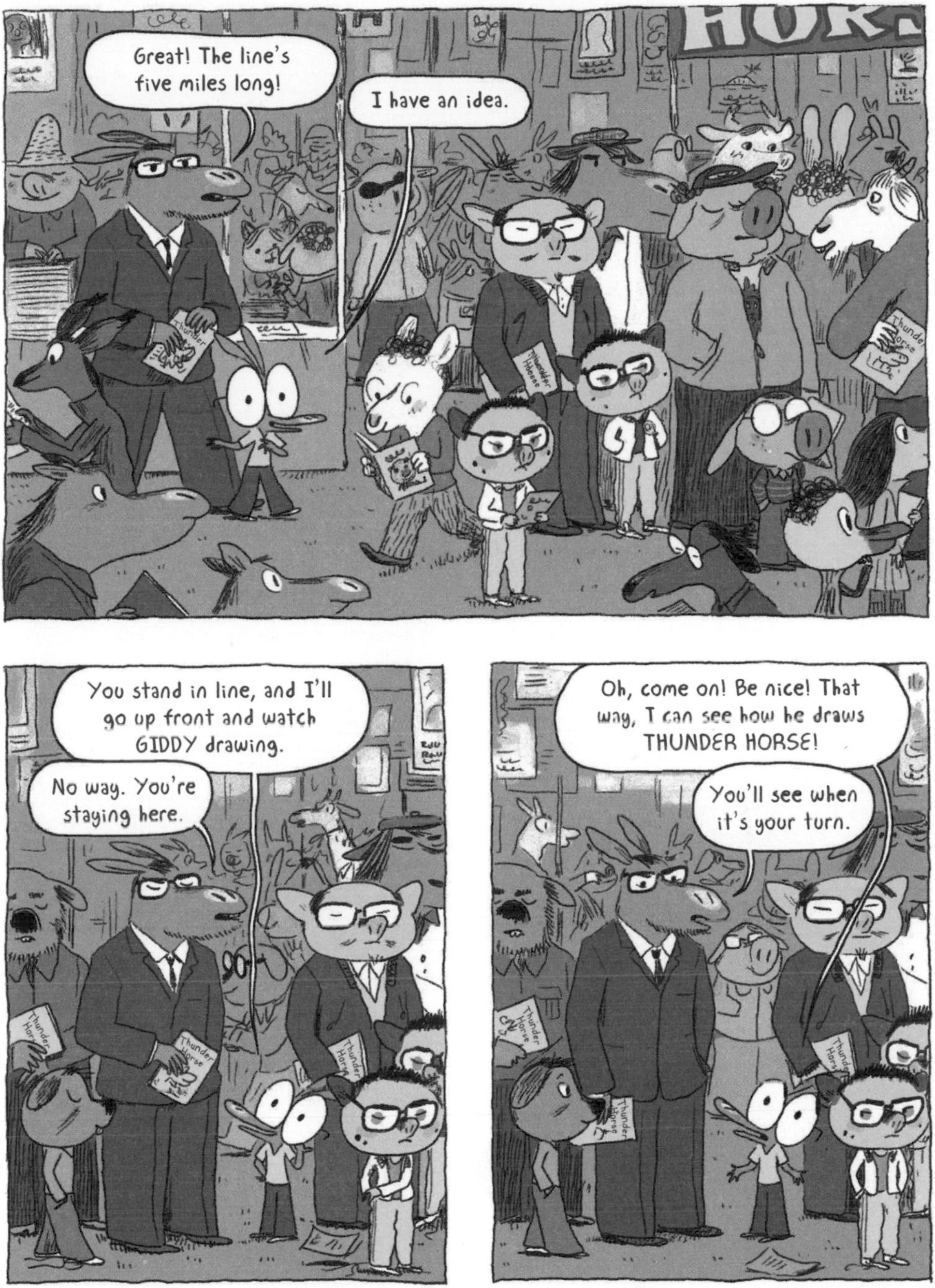
HOR
Great! The line's five miles long!
I have an idea.
Thunder
Thunder Horse
Thunder Horse
You stand in line, and I'll go up front and watch GIDDY drawing.
No way. You're staying here.
Thunder Horse
Thunder Horse
Thunder Horse
Oh, come on! Be nice! That way, I can see how he draws THUNDER HORSE!
You'll see when it's your turn.
Thunder Horse
Thunder Horse
Thunder Horse

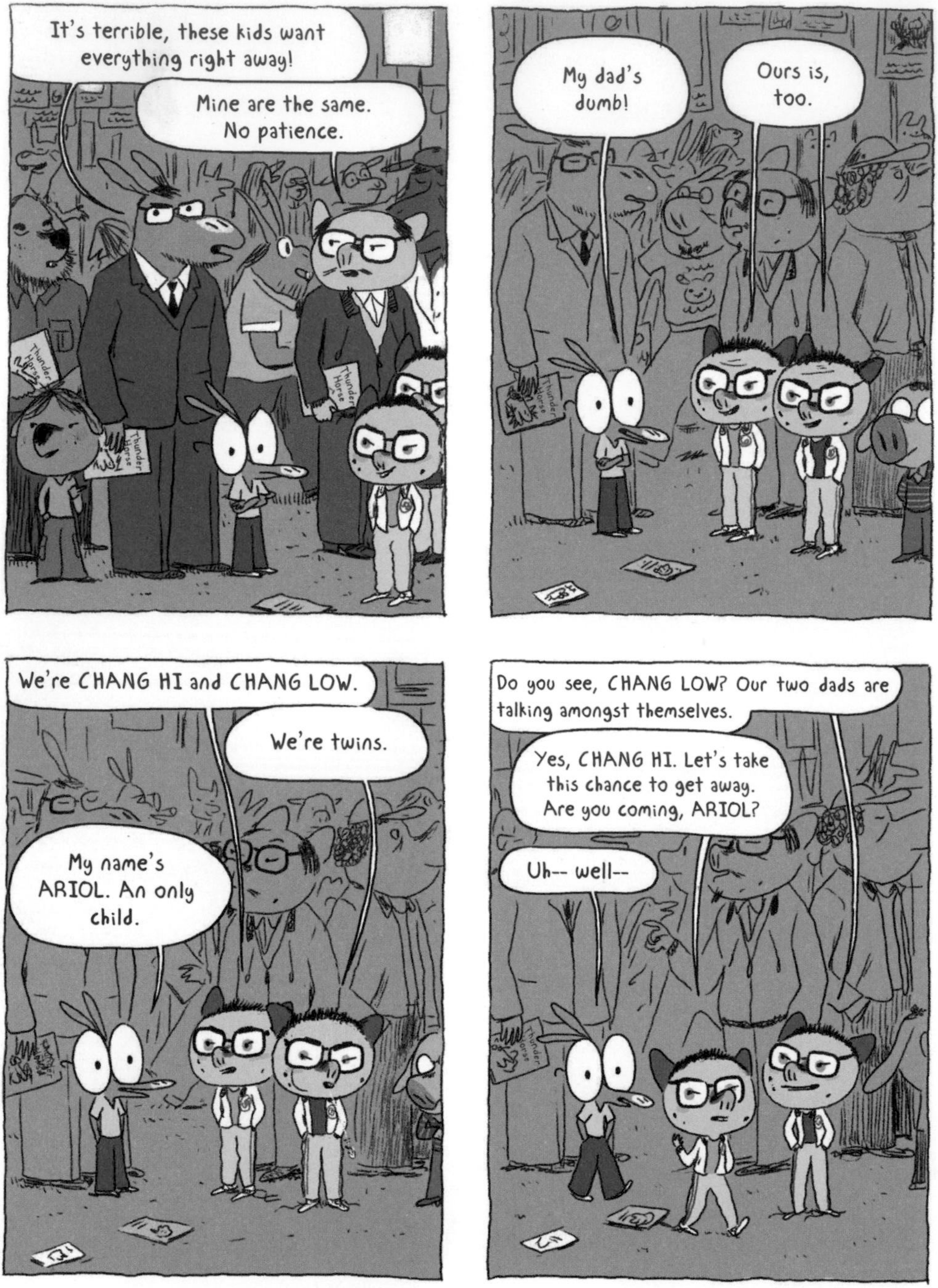
It's terrible, these kids want everything right away!
Mine are the same. No patience.
My dad's dumb!
Ours is, too.
We're CHANG HI and CHANG LOW.
We're twins.
My name's ARIOL. An only child.
Do you see, CHANG LOW? Our two dads are talking amongst themselves.
Yes, CHANG HI. Let's take this chance to get away. Are you coming, ARIOL?
Uh-- well--

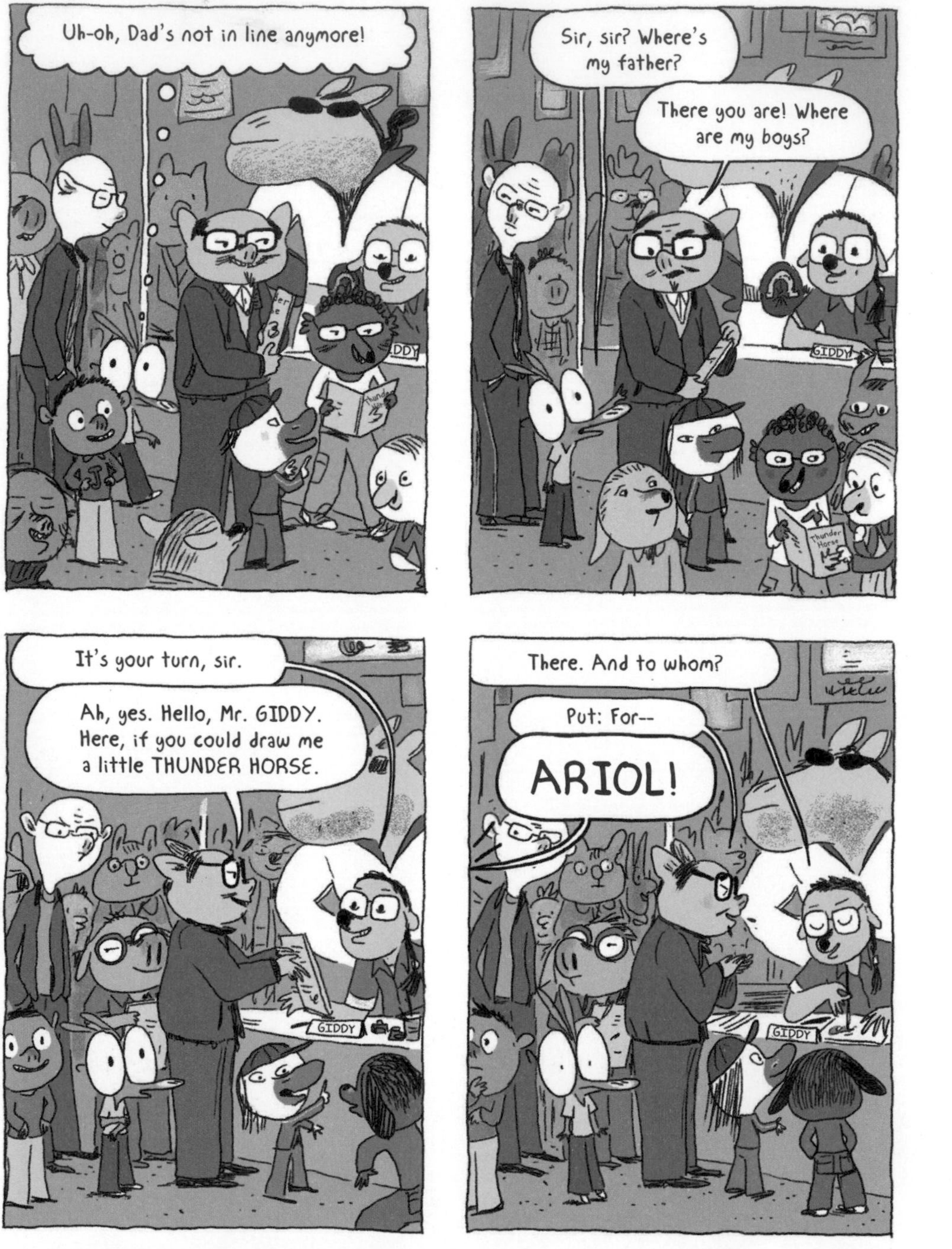
Uh-oh, Dad's not in line anymore!
GIDDY
Sir, sir? Where's my father?
There you are! Where are my boys?
GIDDY
Thunder Horse
It's your turn, sir.
Ah, yes. Hello, Mr. GIDDY. Here, if you could draw me a little THUNDER HORSE.
GIDDY
There. And to whom?
Put: For--
ARIOL!
GIDDY

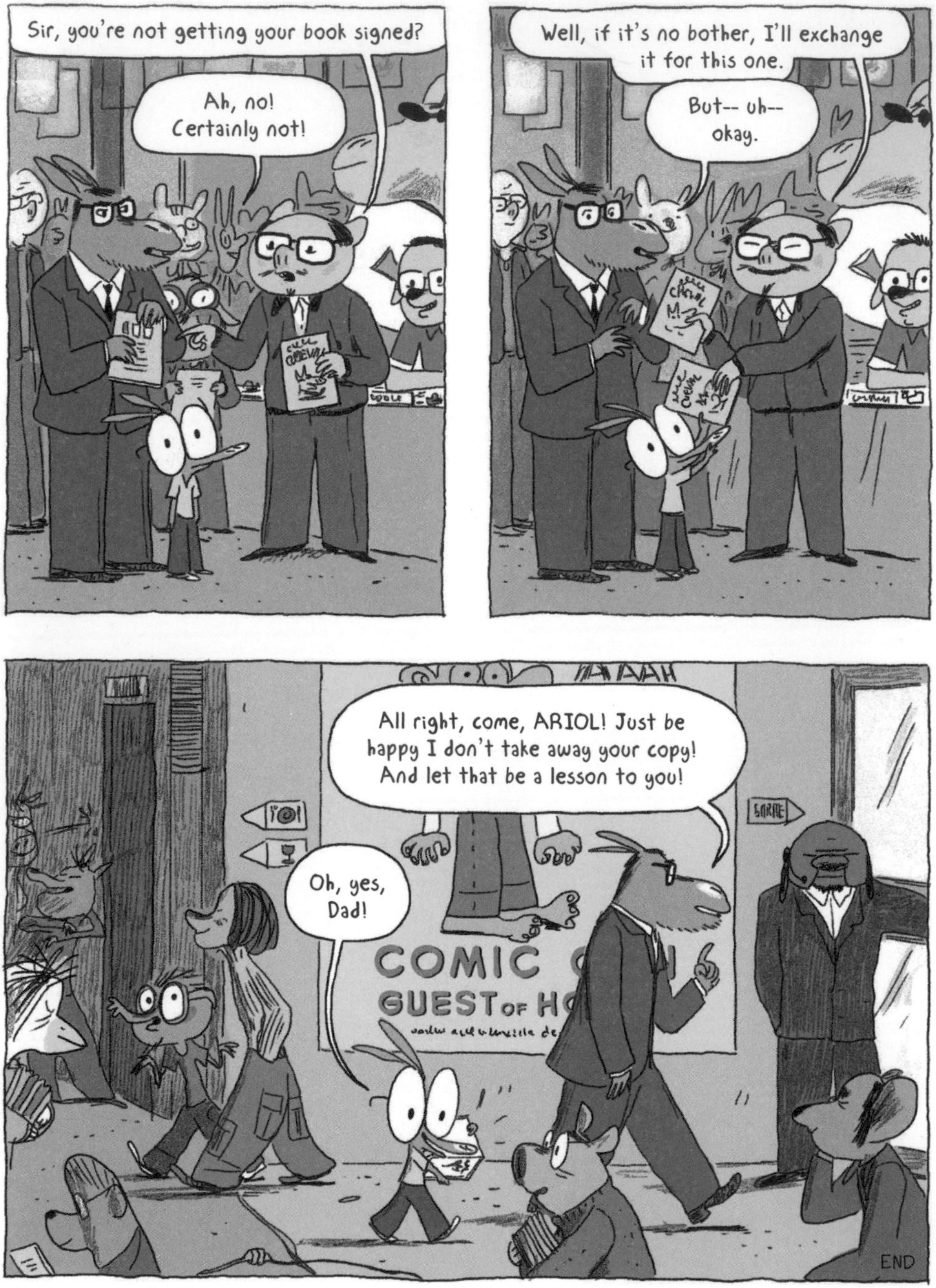
Sir, you're not getting your book signed?
Ah, no! Certainly not!
Well, if it's no bother, I'll exchange it for this one.
But-- uh-- okay.
All right, come, ARIOL! Just be happy I don't take away your copy! And let that be a lesson to you!
Oh, yes, Dad!
END

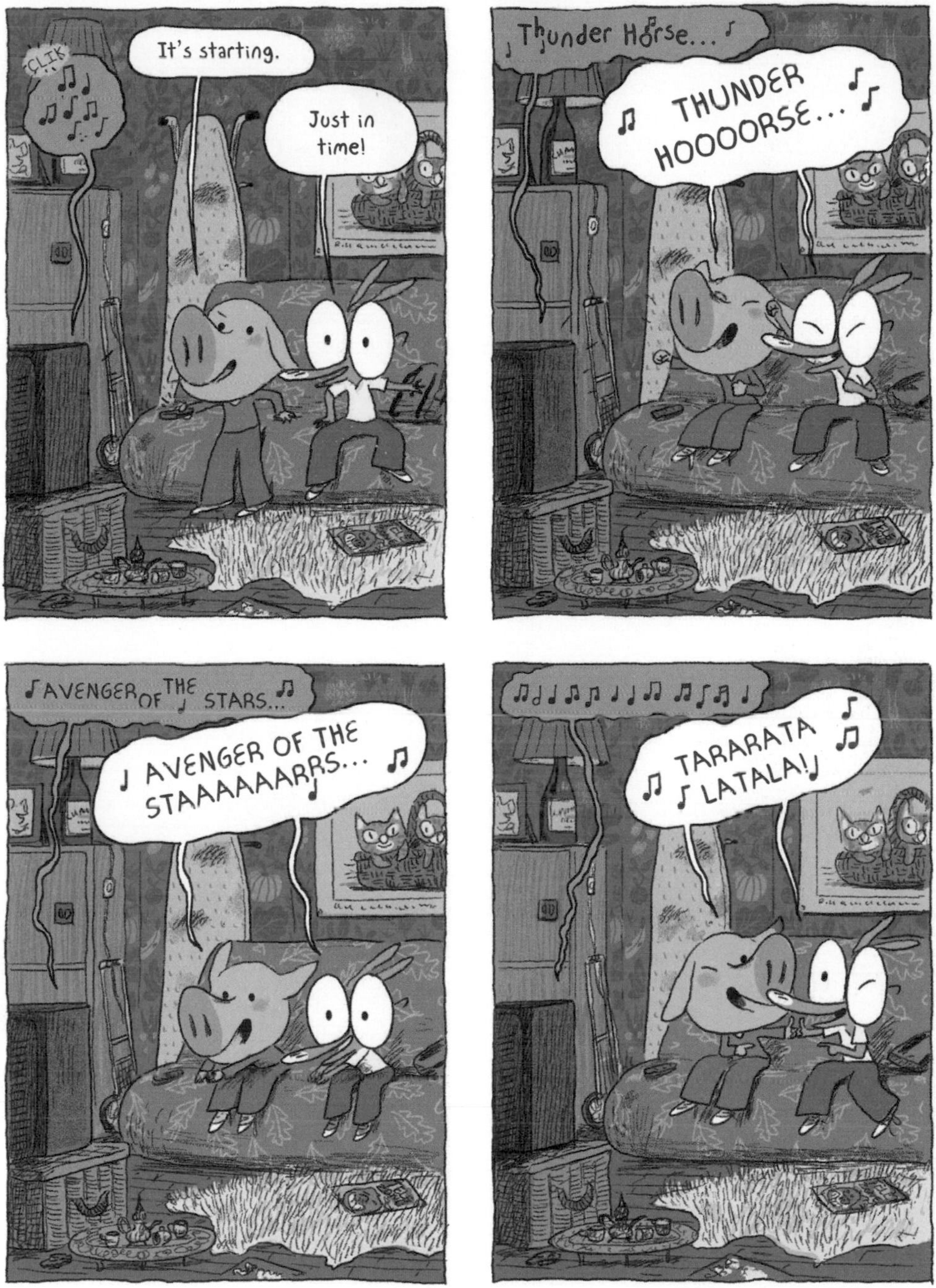
CLIK
It's starting.
Just in time!
Thunder Horse...
THUNDER HOOOORSE...
AVENGER OF THE STARS...
AVENGER OF THE STAAAAAARRS...
TARARATA LATALA!

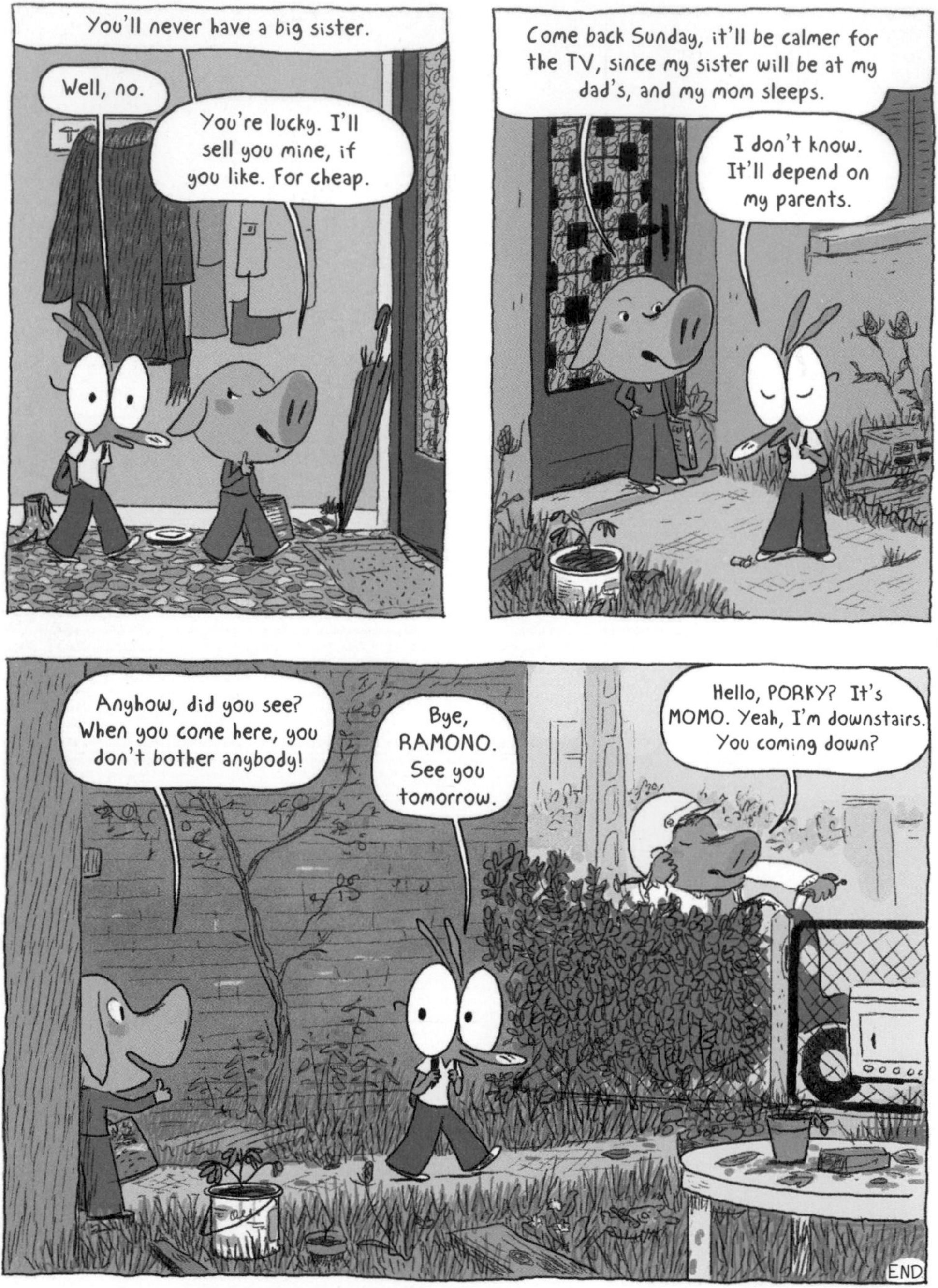
You'll never have a big sister.
Well, no.
You're lucky. I'll sell you mine, if you like. For cheap.
Come back Sunday, it'll be calmer for the TV, since my sister will be at my dad's, and my mom sleeps.
I don't know. It'll depend on my parents.
Anyhow, did you see? When you come here, you don't bother anybody!
Bye, RAMONO. See you tomorrow.
Hello, PORKY? It's MOMO. Yeah, I'm downstairs. You coming down?
END

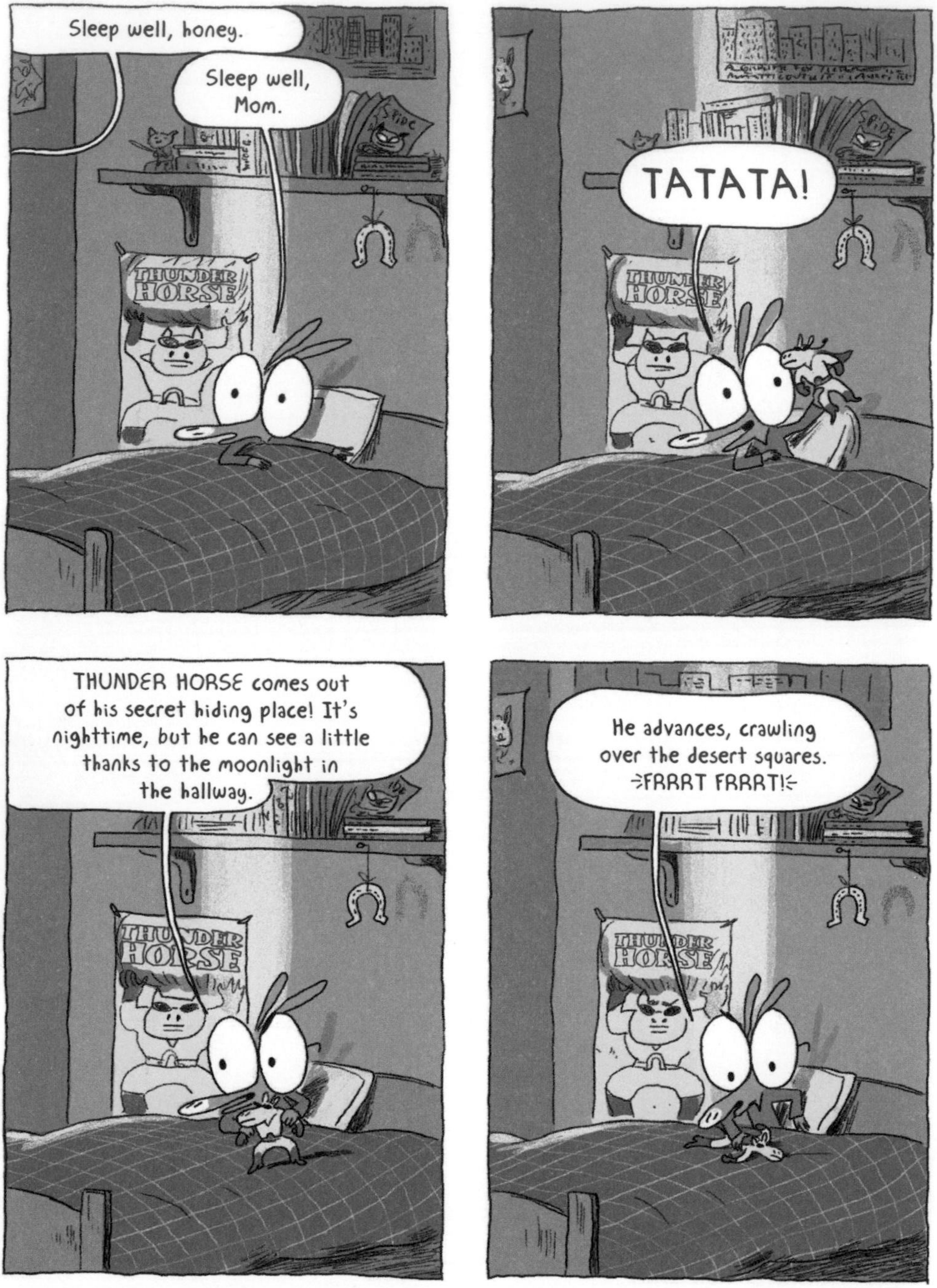
Sleep well, honey.
Sleep well, Mom.
TATATA!
THUNDER HORSE comes out of his secret hiding place! It's nighttime, but he can see a little thanks to the moonlight in the hallway.
He advances, crawling over the desert squares. FRRRT FRRRT!

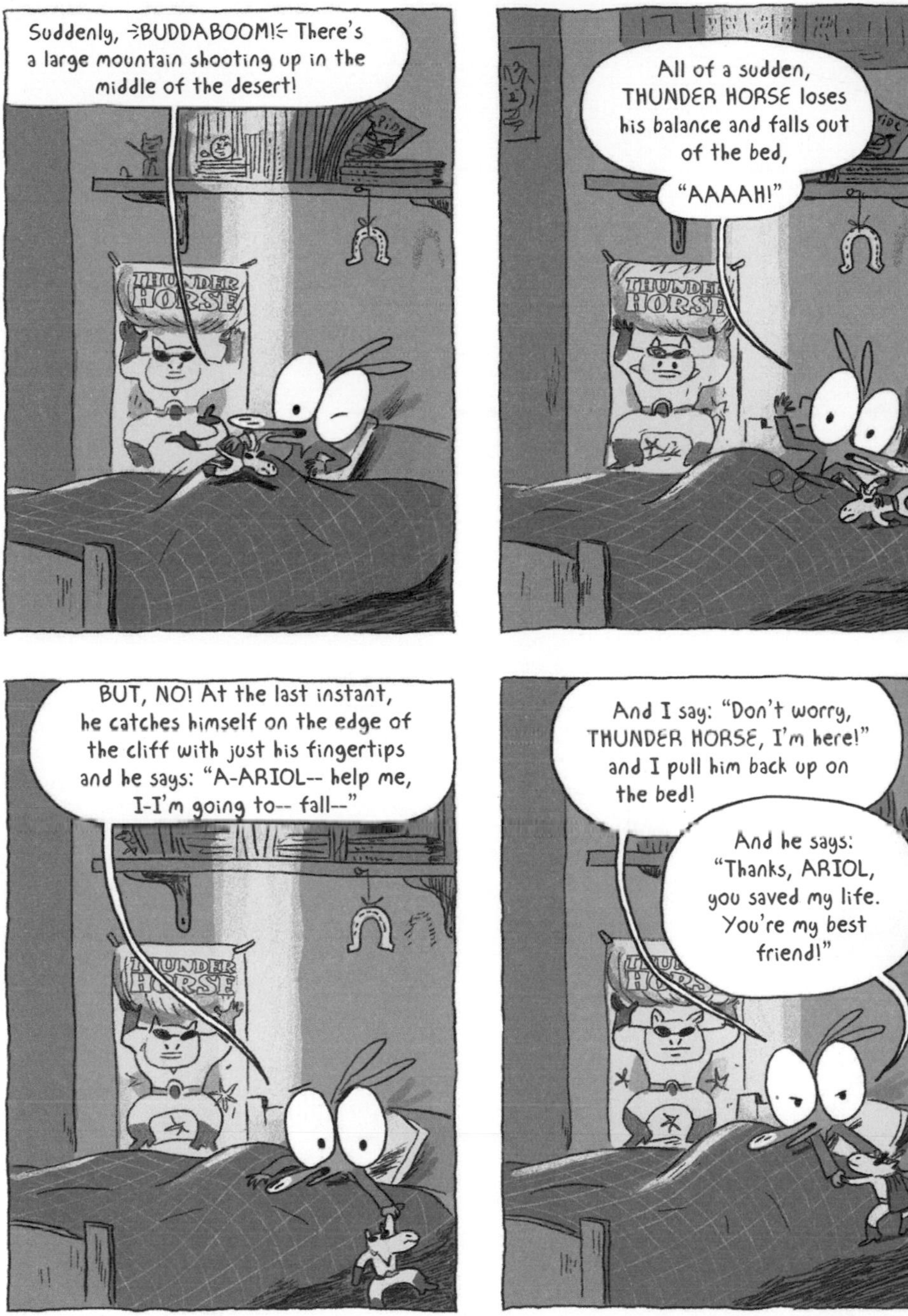
Suddenly, ⇒BUDDABOOM!⇐ There's a large mountain shooting up in the middle of the desert!
All of a sudden, THUNDER HORSE loses his balance and falls out of the bed,
"AAAAH!"
BUT, NO! At the last instant, he catches himself on the edge of the cliff with just his fingertips and he says: "A-ARIOL-- help me, I-I'm going to-- fall--"
And I say: "Don't worry, THUNDER HORSE, I'm here!" and I pull him back up on the bed!
And he says: "Thanks, ARIOL, you saved my life. You're my best friend!"
THUNDER HORSE

And then, THUNDER HORSE starts to climb the mountain, ⇒CLOP CLOP CLOP!⇐

What he doesn't know is that, on the other side of the mountain, TATATA!, his enemy is there, the EMPEROR MORODAN, who's hiding out.

And when THUNDER HORSE reaches the summit, the EMPEROR MORODAN leaps out and says: "HAHA! I WAS WAITING FOR YOU, THUNDER HORSE!"

AND POW! They start to battle one another ⇒BONG! RLAH! AAARG!⇐

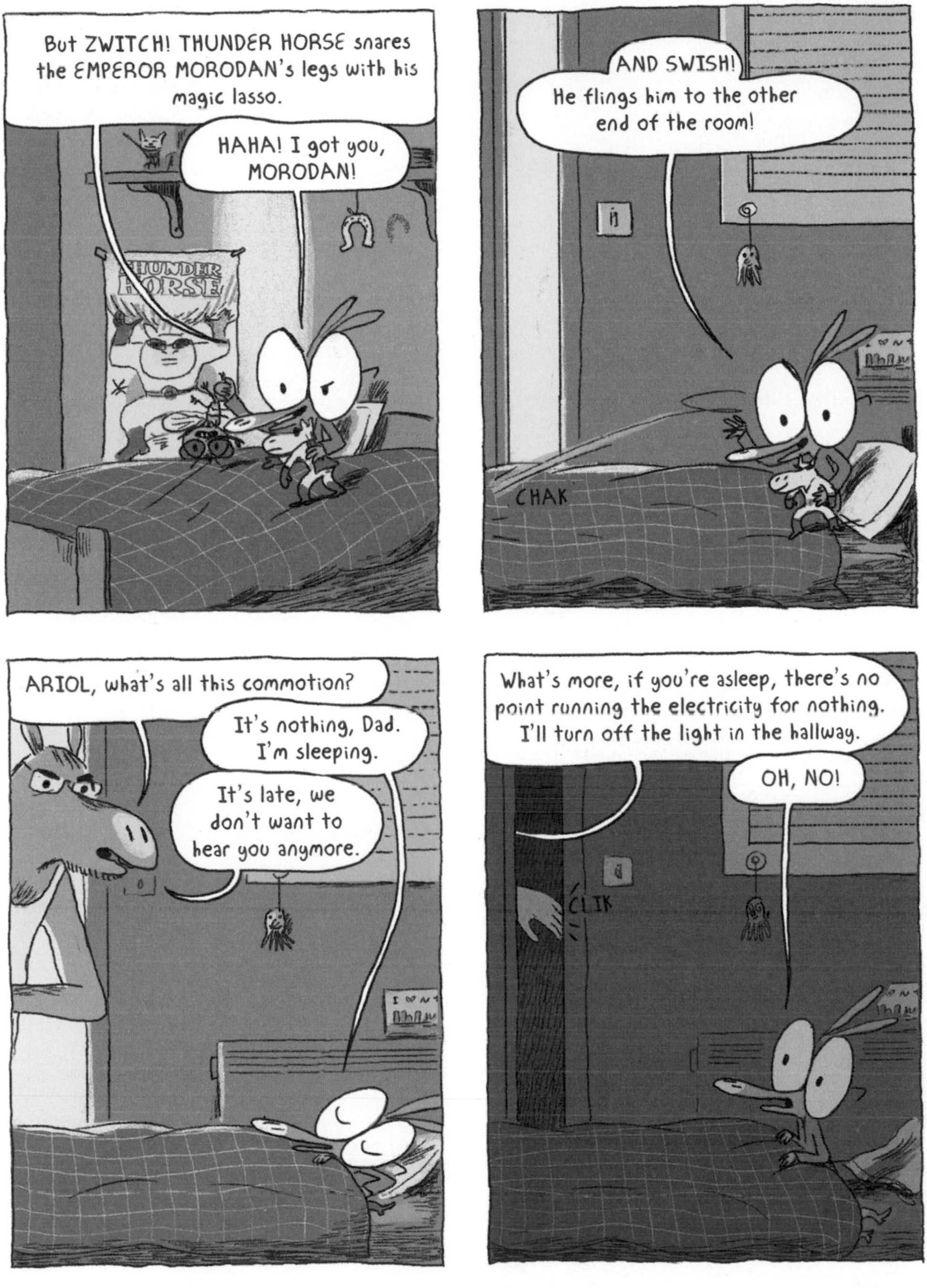

But ZWITCH! THUNDER HORSE snares the EMPEROR MORODAN's legs with his magic lasso.
HAHA! I got you, MORODAN!
THUNDER HORSE
AND SWISH!
He flings him to the other end of the room!
CHAK
ARIOL, what's all this commotion?
It's nothing, Dad. I'm sleeping.
It's late, we don't want to hear you anymore.
What's more, if you're asleep, there's no point running the electricity for nothing. I'll turn off the light in the hallway.
OH, NO!
CLIK

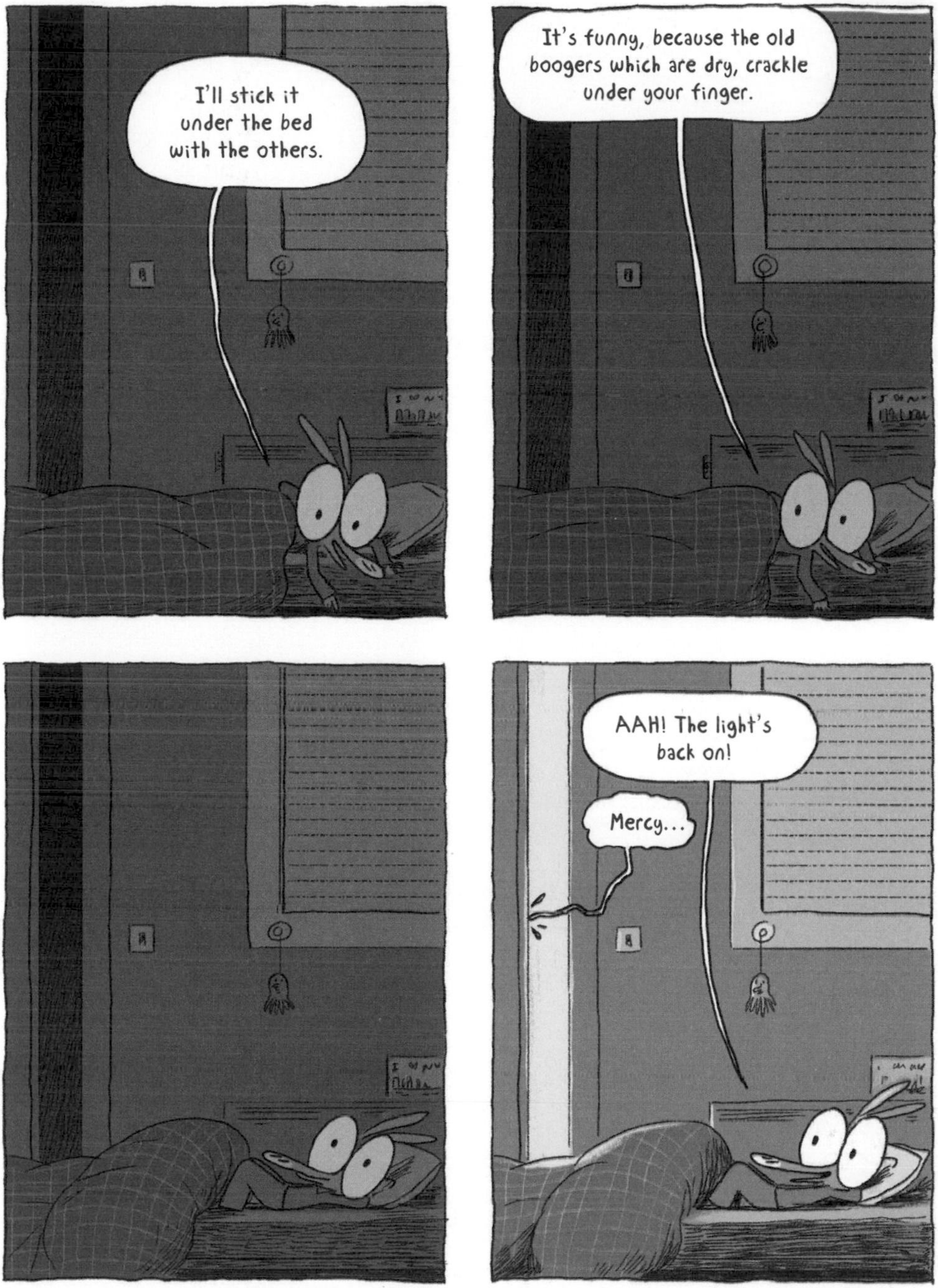
I'll stick it under the bed with the others.
It's funny, because the old boogers which are dry, crackle under your finger.
AAH! The light's back on!
Mercy...

ARIOL

Granny in the Subway

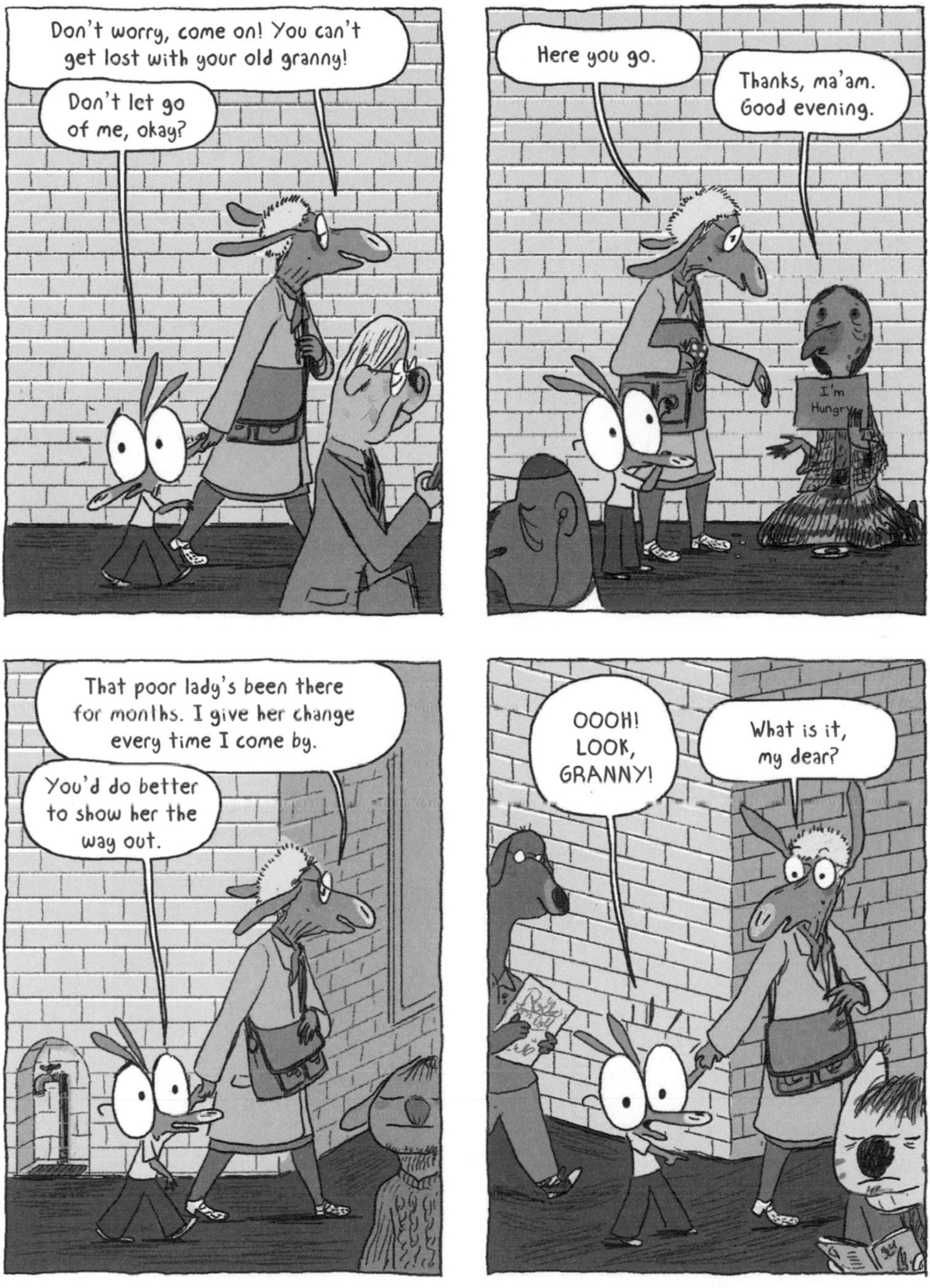
Don't worry, come on! You can't get lost with your old granny!
Don't let go of me, okay?
Here you go.
Thanks, ma'am. Good evening.
I'm Hungry
That poor lady's been there for months. I give her change every time I come by.
You'd do better to show her the way out.
OOOH! LOOK, GRANNY!
What is it, my dear?

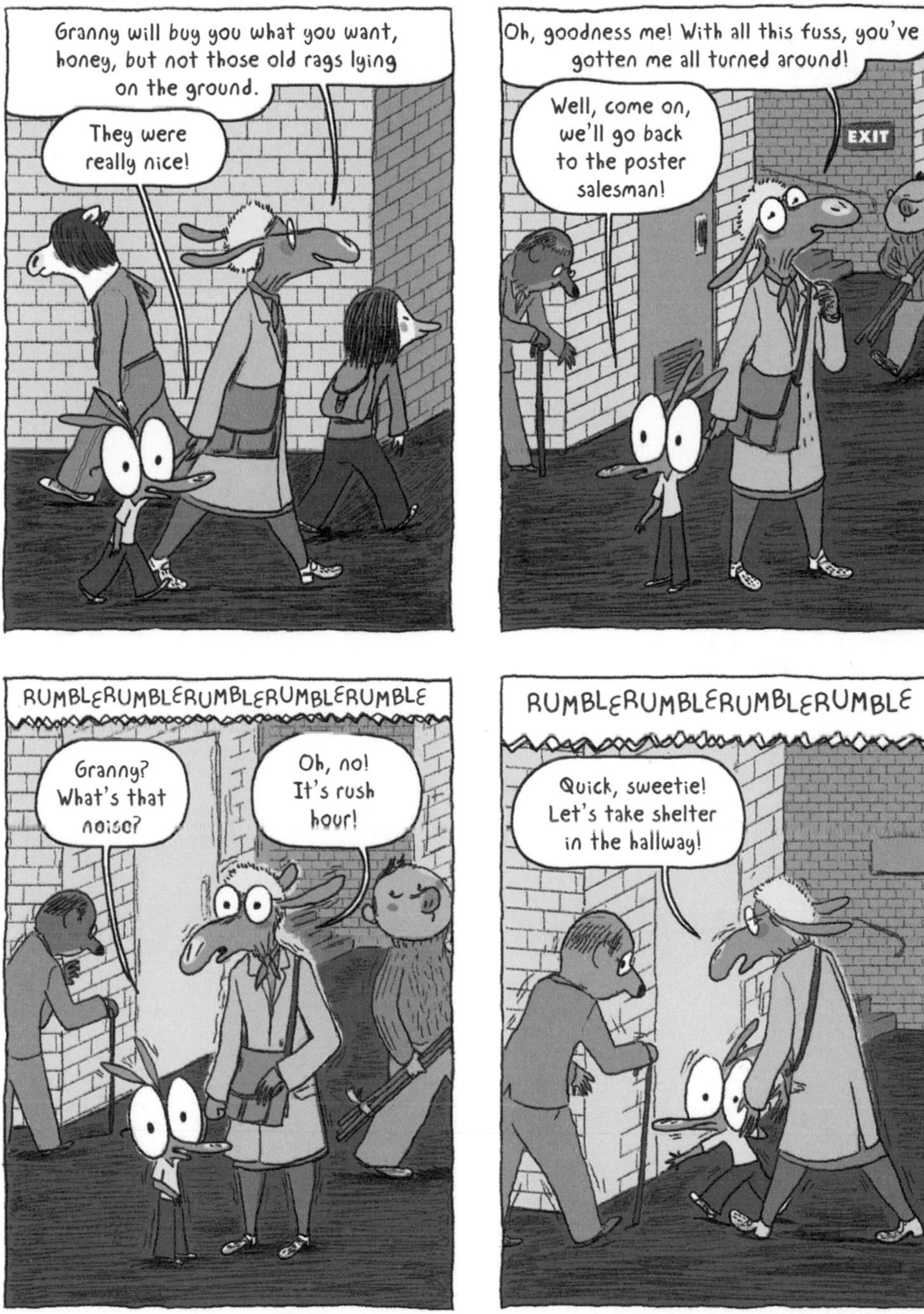
Granny will buy you what you want, honey, but not those old rags lying on the ground.
They were really nice!
Oh, goodness me! With all this fuss, you've gotten me all turned around!
Well, come on, we'll go back to the poster salesman!
EXIT
RUMBLERUMBLERUMBLERUMBLERUMBLE
Granny? What's that noise?
Oh, no! It's rush hour!
RUMBLERUMBLERUMBLERUMBLE
Quick, sweetie! Let's take shelter in the hallway!

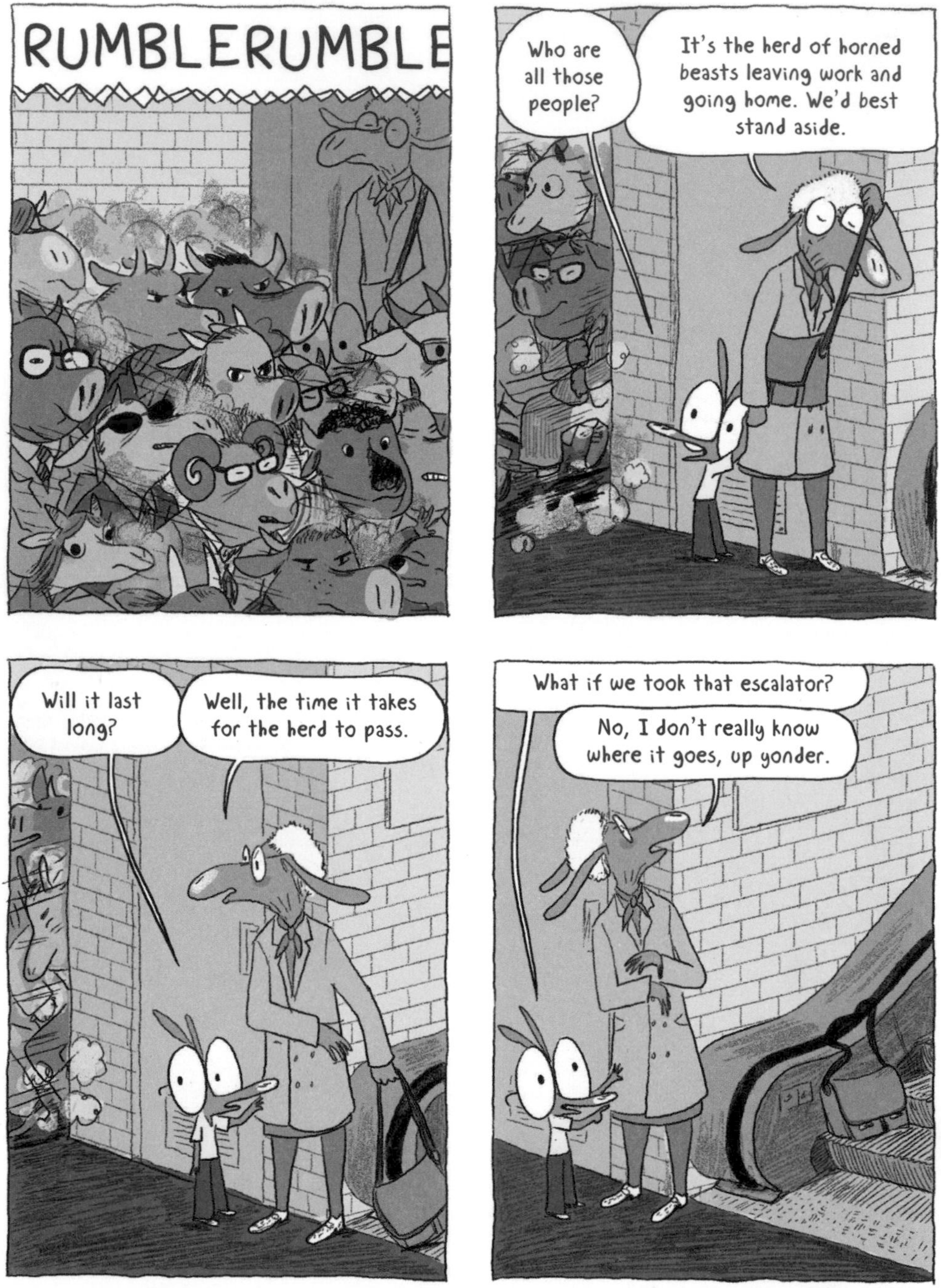
RUMBLERUMBLE
Who are all those people?
It's the herd of horned beasts leaving work and going home. We'd best stand aside.
Will it last long?
Well, the time it takes for the herd to pass.
What if we took that escalator?
No, I don't really know where it goes, up yonder.

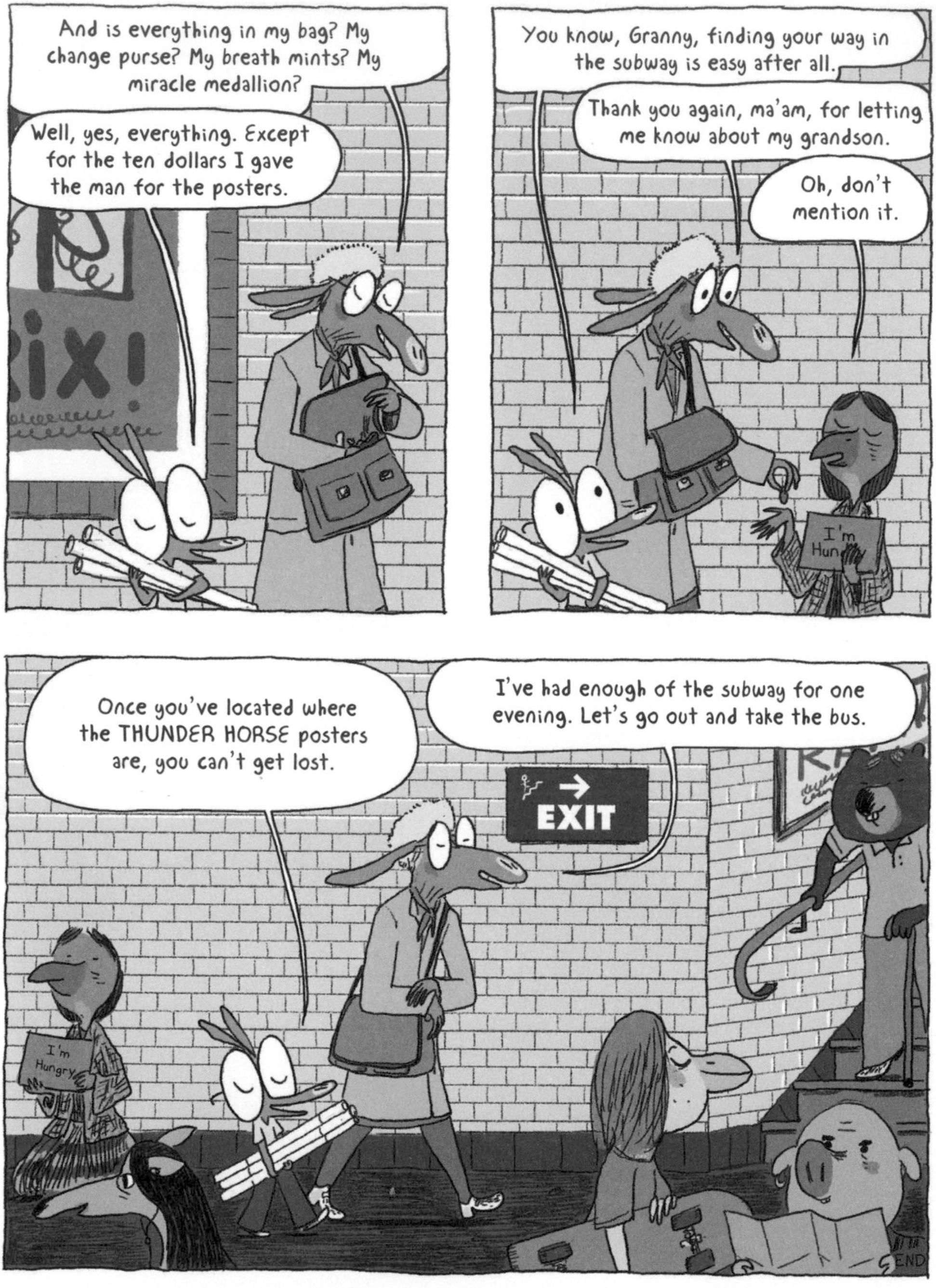
And is everything in my bag? My change purse? My breath mints? My miracle medallion?
Well, yes, everything. Except for the ten dollars I gave the man for the posters.
You know, Granny, finding your way in the subway is easy after all.
Thank you again, ma'am, for letting me know about my grandson.
Oh, don't mention it.
I'm Hun
Once you've located where the THUNDER HORSE posters are, you can't get lost.
I've had enough of the subway for one evening. Let's go out and take the bus.
EXIT
I'm Hungry
END

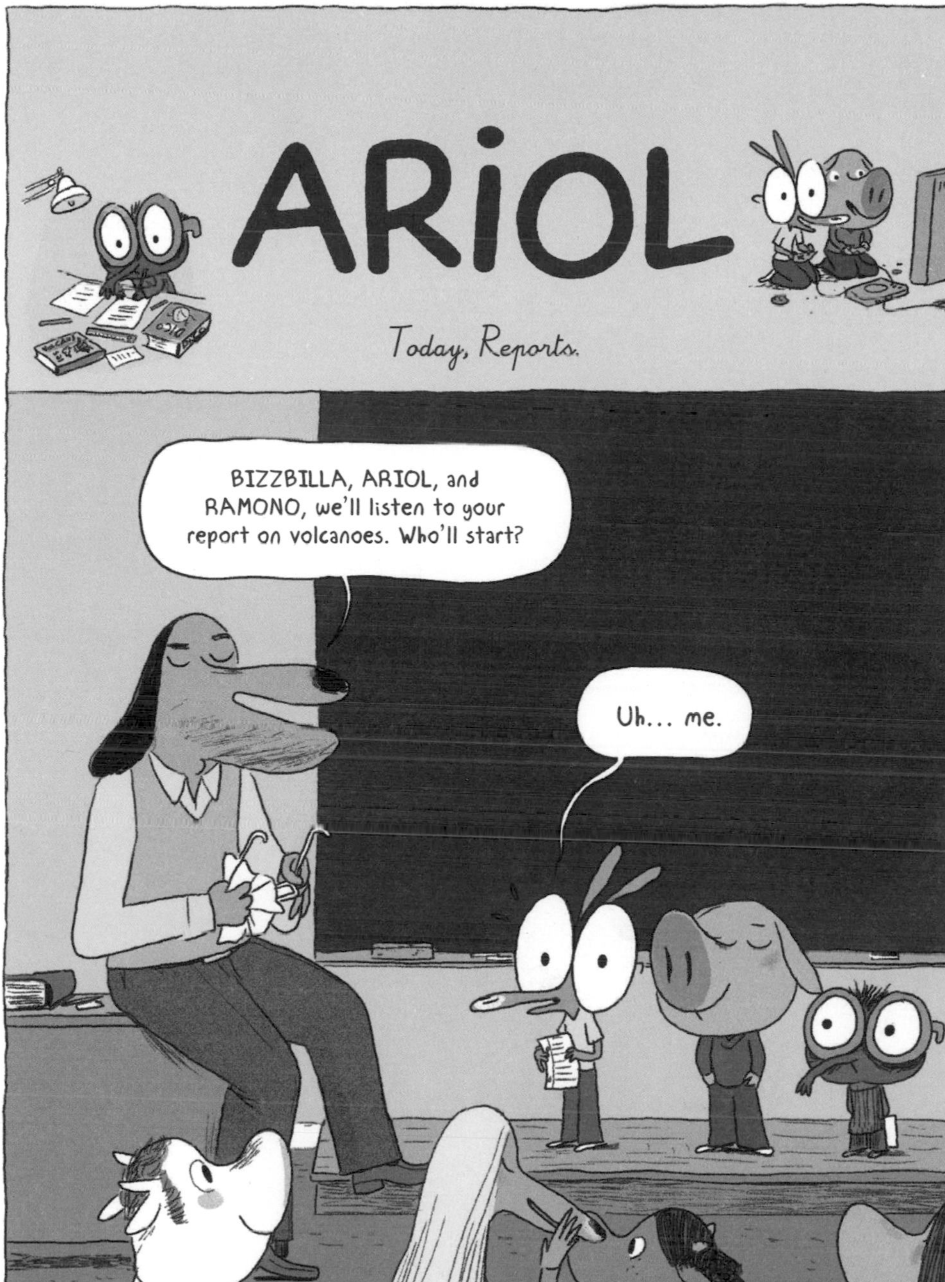
ARiOL
Today, Reports.
BIZZBILLA, ARIOL, and RAMONO, we'll listen to your report on volcanoes. Who'll start?
Uh... me.

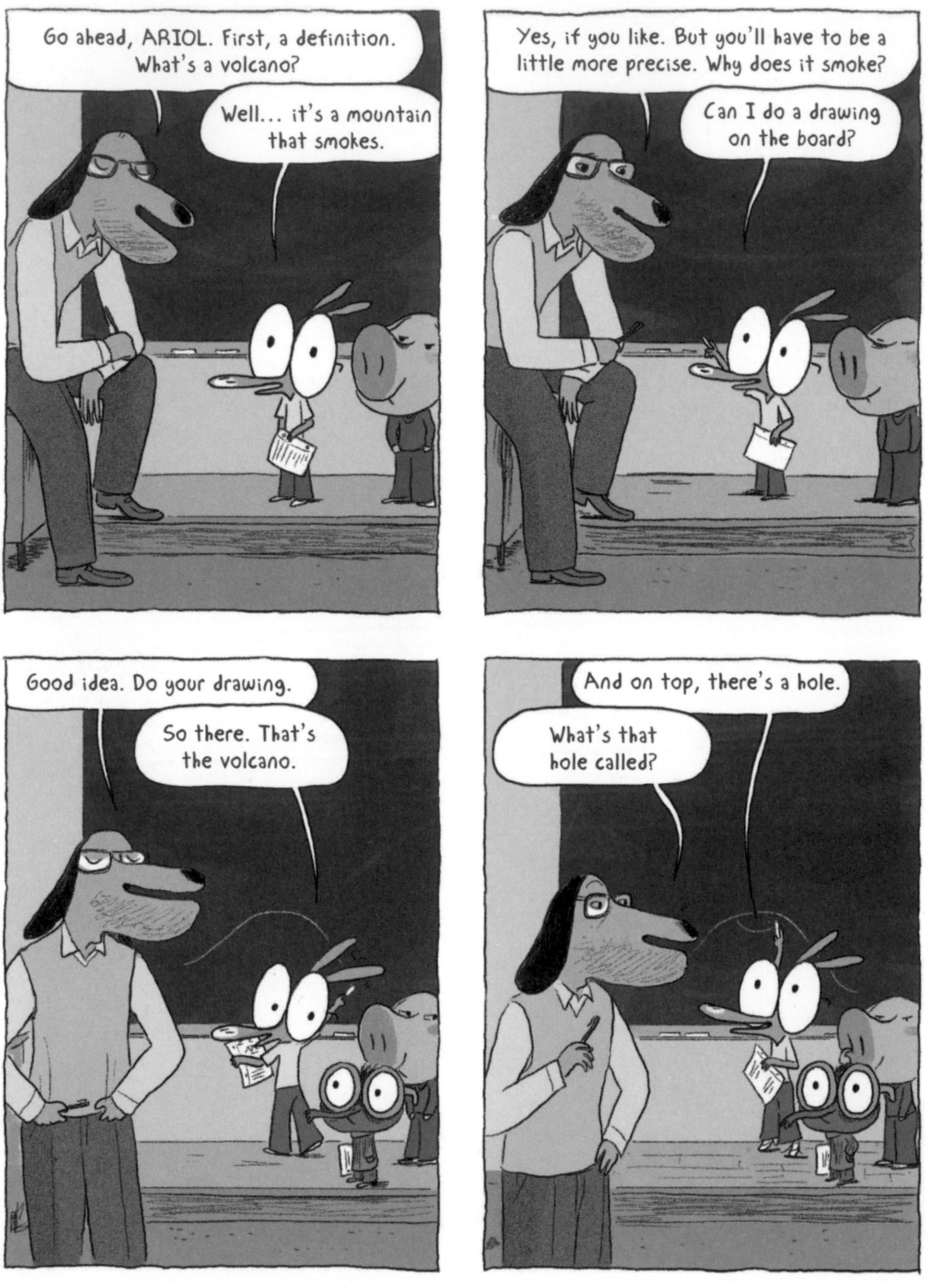
Go ahead, ARIOL. First, a definition. What's a volcano?
Well... it's a mountain that smokes.
Yes, if you like. But you'll have to be a little more precise. Why does it smoke?
Can I do a drawing on the board?
Good idea. Do your drawing.
So there. That's the volcano.
And on top, there's a hole.
What's that hole called?

AAAH! That's better! Well, this fire is called MAGMA. And you mustn't touch it, or else you'll get burned!

CRATER

CHIMNEY

And now, I'll pass the mike to BIZZBILLA, who's going to talk to you about irruptions.

E-ruptions, RAMONO. Your report was done pretty fast! Write MAGMA on the board then.

CRATER

CHIMNEY

Right away. But before that, I'll put my sweater back on because I'm a little cold now.

⇒Pssst!⇐
BIZZBILLA!
How do you spell MAGMA?

M-A-G-M-A.

CRATER

CHIMNEY

My turn. I'm going to talk to you about eruptions. A volcano is simple, in fact. It's like a person who has a huge secret she can't say.

CRATER

CHIMNEY

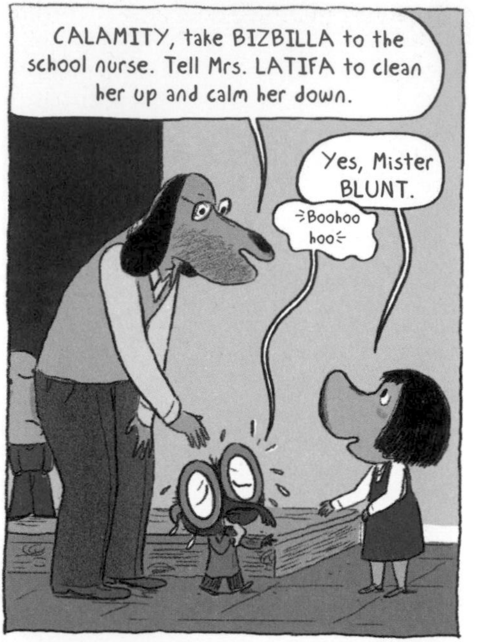

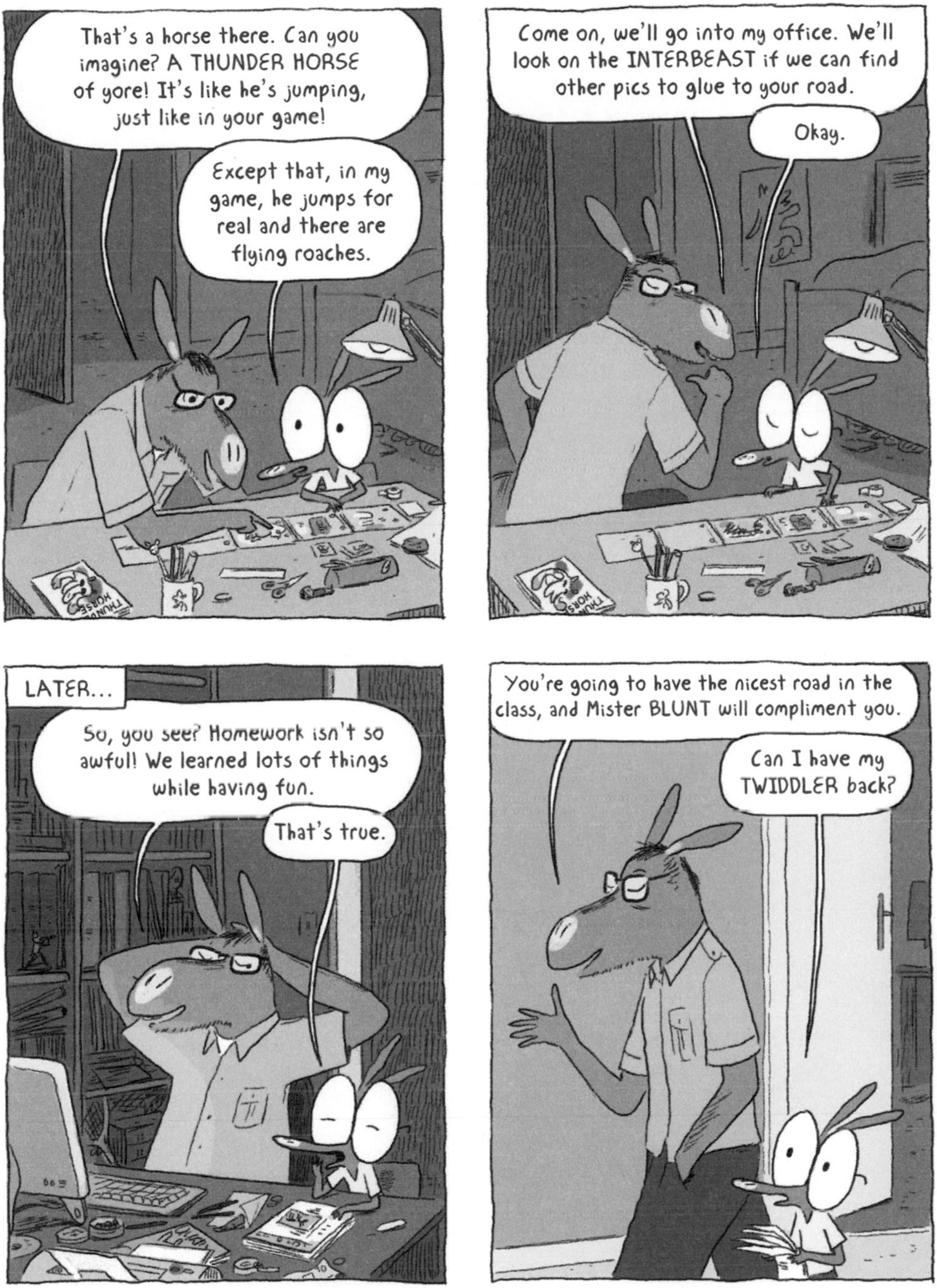
That's a horse there. Can you imagine? A THUNDER HORSE of yore! It's like he's jumping, just like in your game!
Except that, in my game, he jumps for real and there are flying roaches.
Come on, we'll go into my office. We'll look on the INTERBEAST if we can find other pics to glue to your road.
Okay.
LATER...
So, you see? Homework isn't so awful! We learned lots of things while having fun.
That's true.
You're going to have the nicest road in the class, and Mister BLUNT will compliment you.
Can I have my TWIDDLER back?

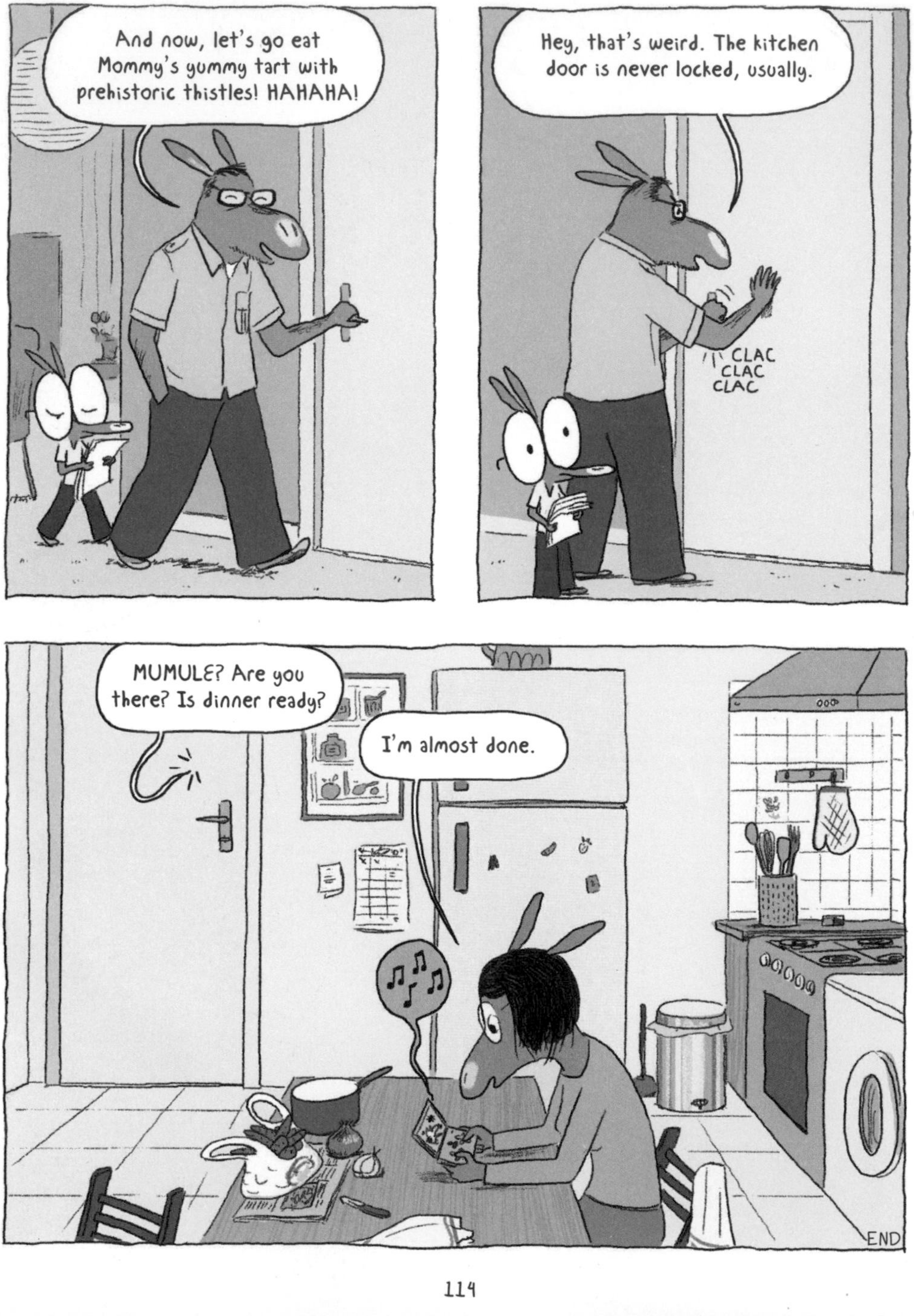
And now, let's go eat Mommy's yummy tart with prehistoric thistles! HAHAHA!
Hey, that's weird. The kitchen door is never locked, usually.
CLAC CLAC CLAC
MUMULE? Are you there? Is dinner ready?
I'm almost done.
END

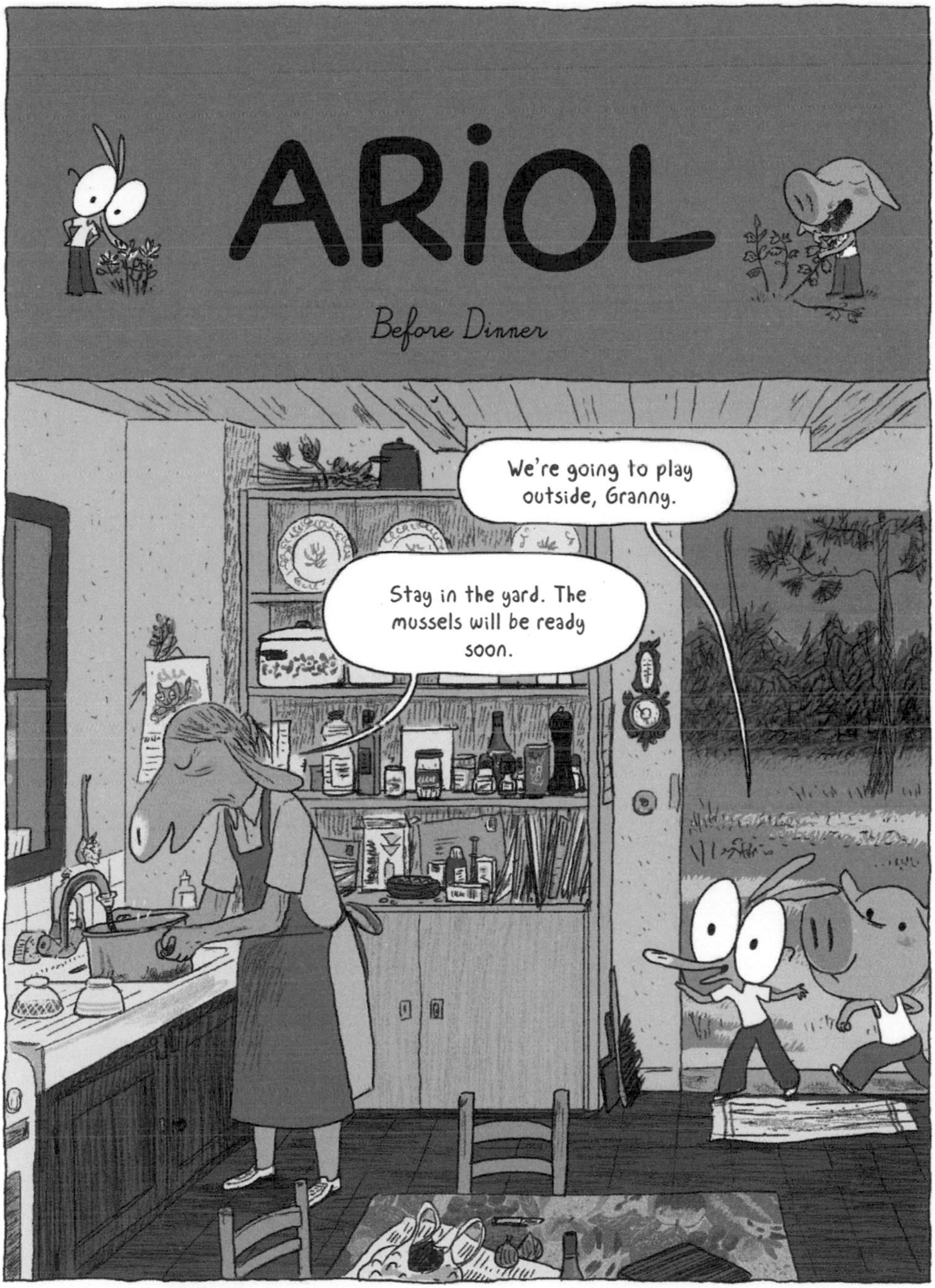
ARiOL
Before Dinner
We're going to play outside, Granny.
Stay in the yard. The mussels will be ready soon.

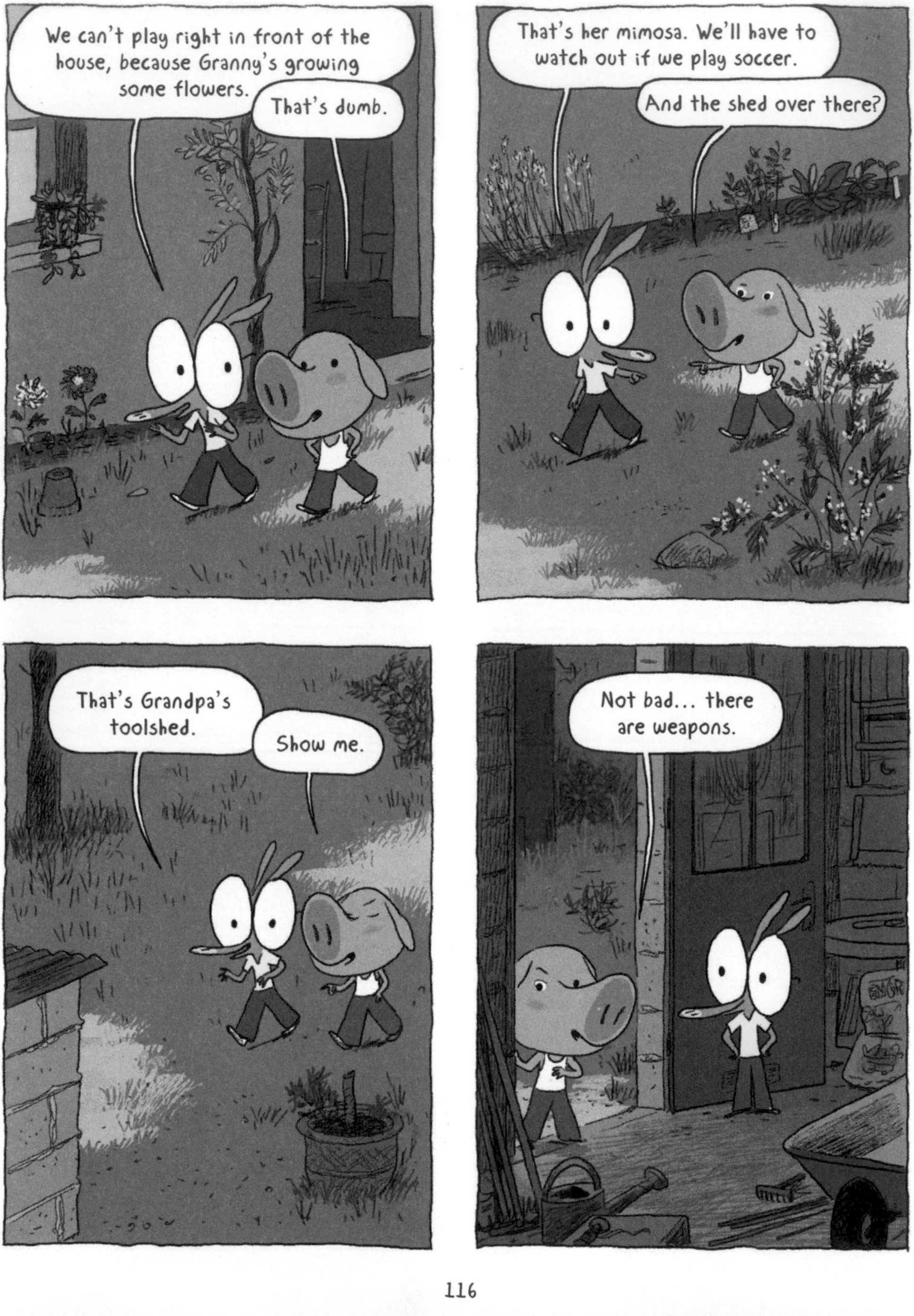

We can't play right in front of the house, because Granny's growing some flowers.
That's dumb.
That's her mimosa. We'll have to watch out if we play soccer.
And the shed over there?
That's Grandpa's toolshed.
Show me.
Not bad... there are weapons.

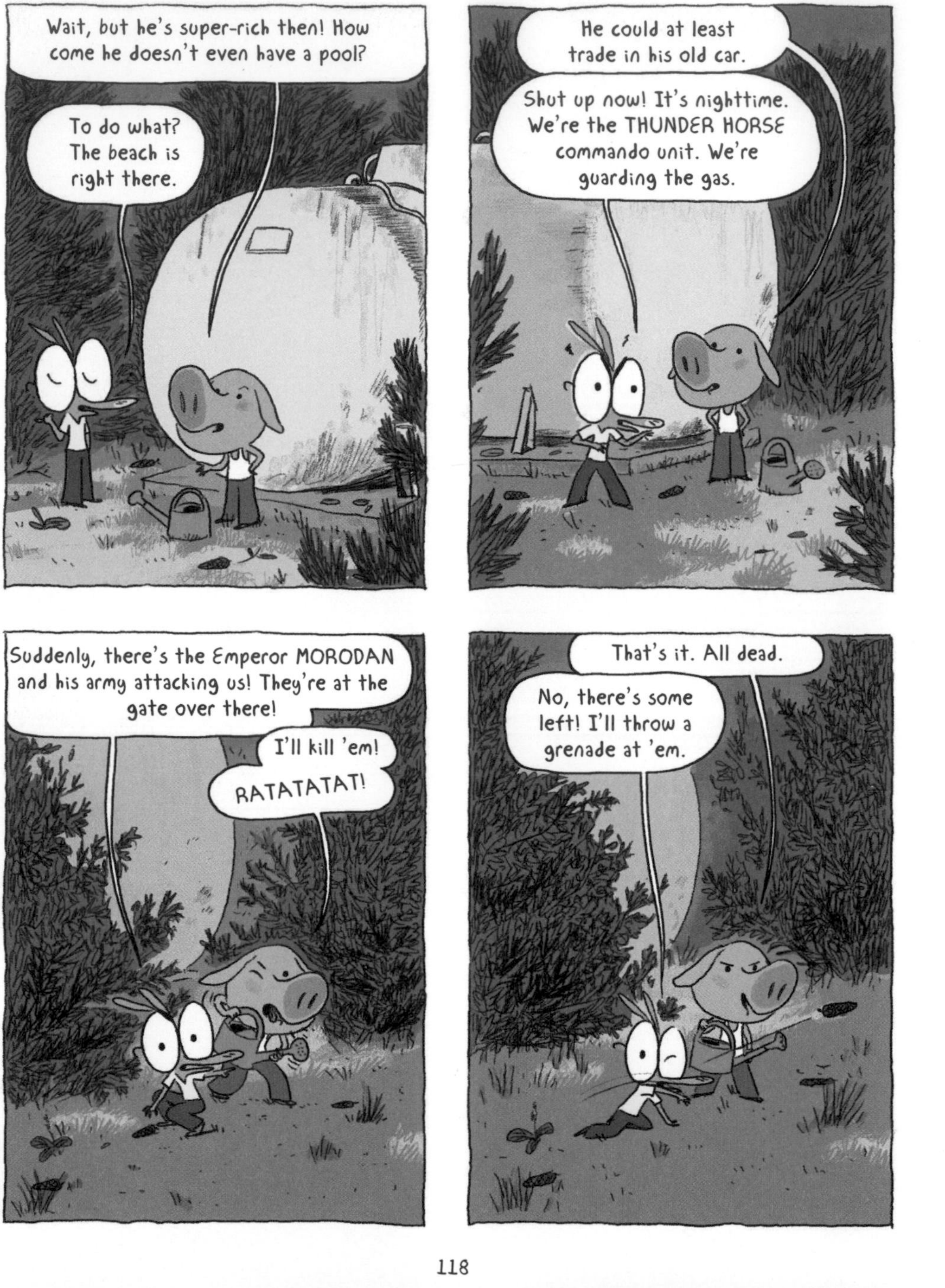

Wait, but he's super-rich then! How come he doesn't even have a pool?
To do what? The beach is right there.
He could at least trade in his old car.
Shut up now! It's nighttime. We're the THUNDER HORSE commando unit. We're guarding the gas.
Suddenly, there's the Emperor MORODAN and his army attacking us! They're at the gate over there!
I'll kill 'em!
RATATATAT!
That's it. All dead.
No, there's some left! I'll throw a grenade at 'em.

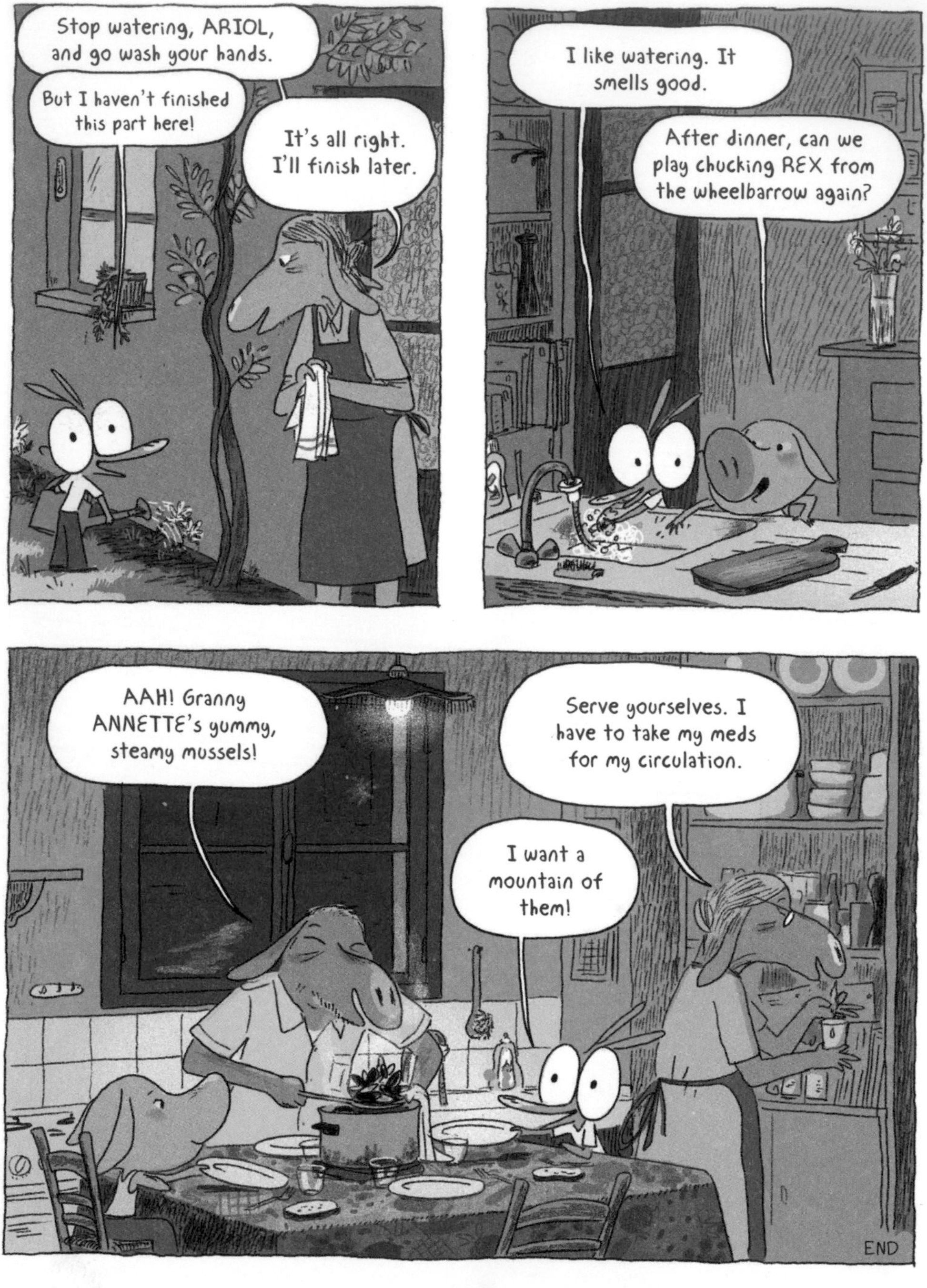
Stop watering, ARIOL, and go wash your hands.
But I haven't finished this part here!
It's all right. I'll finish later.
I like watering. It smells good.
After dinner, can we play chucking REX from the wheelbarrow again?
AAH! Granny ANNETTE's yummy, steamy mussels!
Serve yourselves. I have to take my meds for my circulation.
I want a mountain of them!
END

WATCH OUT FOR PAPERCUTZ

Welcome to the third tender-hearted ARIOL graphic novel by the awesomely talented team of Emmanuel Guibert and Marc Boutavant from Papercutz, those anthropomorphic creatures dedicated to publishing great graphic novels for all ages. I'm Jim Salamander, er, I mean, Jim Salicrup, your bleary-eyed Editor-in-Chief and President of the Giddy Fan Club, here to enlighten you about another Papercutz series (or two)!

First, though, we want to mention how happy we are that ARIOL has seemed to find an audience so quickly in America. The first two volumes of ARIOL are already back to press for second printings, and that's great news for all ARIOL fans, as that means we get to keep publishing this wonderful series!

As I was looking over the stories for this volume, it struck me how focused it was on the simple joys of everyday life. We see ARIOL with his parents, his grandparents, his friends, and at school and at play. While many other Papercutz graphic novels also feature such scenes, ARIOL is all about that stuff, the other titles focus on mysteries or far-out adventures and include everyday elements as a bonus. We'll see, for example, Nancy Drew (in NANCY DREW AND THE CLUE CREW) spend time with her dad and Mrs. Gruen, her best friends Bess and George, and even see her at school, but Nancy is forever solving mysteries! Even Garfield (in THE GARFIELD SHOW) spends time with friends and family, but still will wind up battling lasagna-like aliens from Outer Space (we're not kidding)!

But there is another Papercutz series that does come very close to ARIOL, and also captures the magic of everyday family life. While in ARIOL, the characters all are animal-like creatures, in ERNEST & REBECCA, by Guillame Bianco and Antonello Dalena, Ernest is a magical microbe. But, that's not as big a deal as you might imagine, especially in ERNEST & REBECCA #3 "Grandpa Bug" and #4 "The Land of the Walking Stones." These graphic novels are also brilliantly written, and spectacularly drawn, and present awesome tales of everyday family life that will make you laugh and cry.

Essentially all I'm saying is, if you enjoy ARIOL, we suspect you'll also love ERNEST & REBECCA. But what do I know? After all, I'm just a donkey-- like you!

Thanks,

Jim

STAY IN TOUCH!

EMAIL: salicrup@papercutz.com
WEB: www.papercutz.com
TWITTER: @papercutzgn
FACEBOOK: PAPERCUTZGRAPHICNOVELS
REGULAR MAIL: Papercutz, 160 Broadway, Suite 700, East Wing, New York, NY 10038

Other Great Titles From PAPERCUTZ™

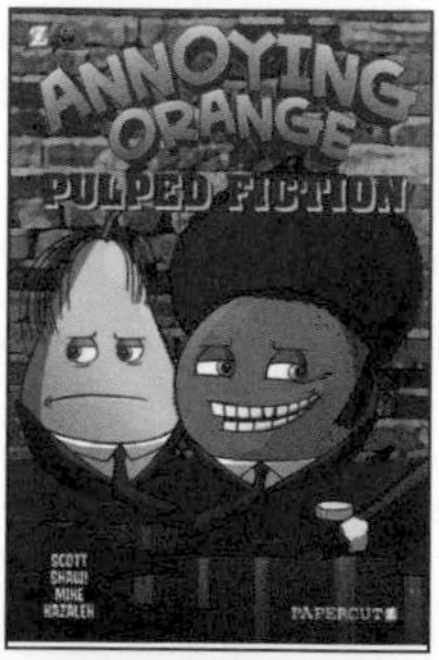
ANNOYING ORANGE
PULPED FICTION
SCOTT SHAW!! MIKE KAZALEH
PAPERCUTZ

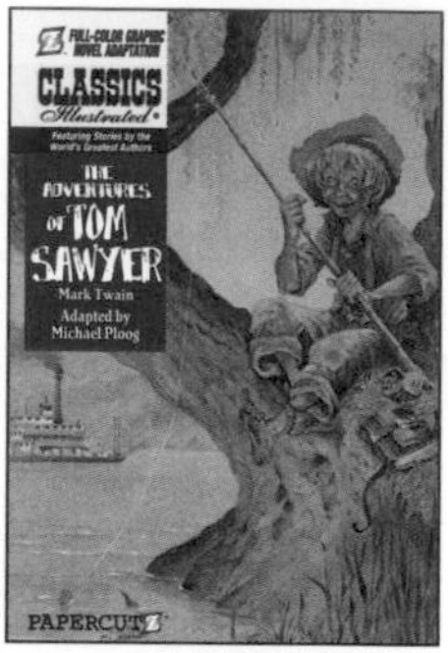
CLASSICS Illustrated
THE ADVENTURES OF TOM SAWYER
Mark Twain
Adapted by Michael Ploog
PAPERCUTZ

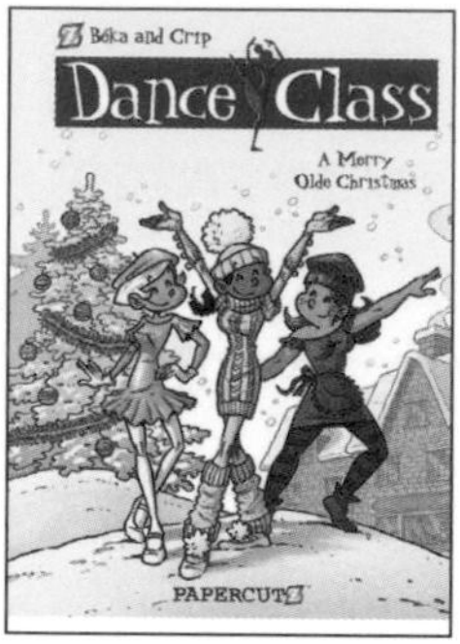
Béka and Crip
Dance Class
A Merry Olde Christmas
PAPERCUTZ

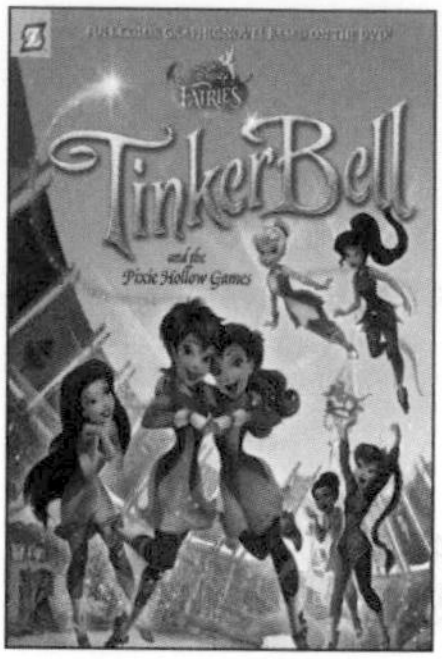
TinkerBell
and the Pixie Hollow Games

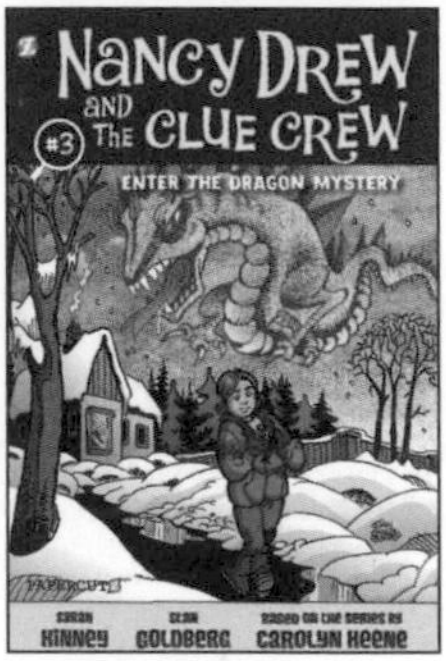
NANCY DREW AND THE CLUE CREW
#3
ENTER THE DRAGON MYSTERY
PAPERCUTZ
KINNEY GOLDBERG CAROLYN KEENE

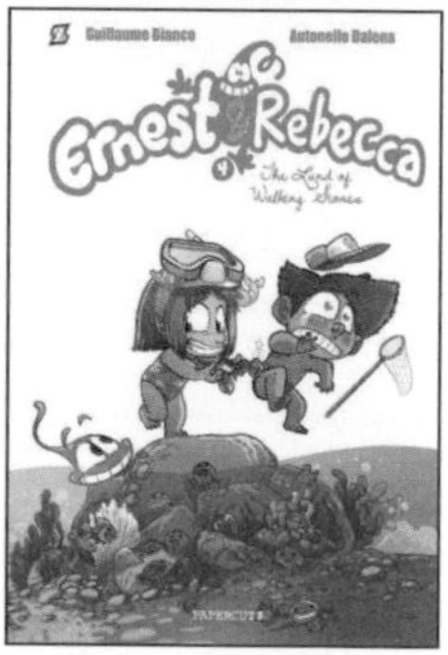
Ernest Rebecca
PAPERCUTZ

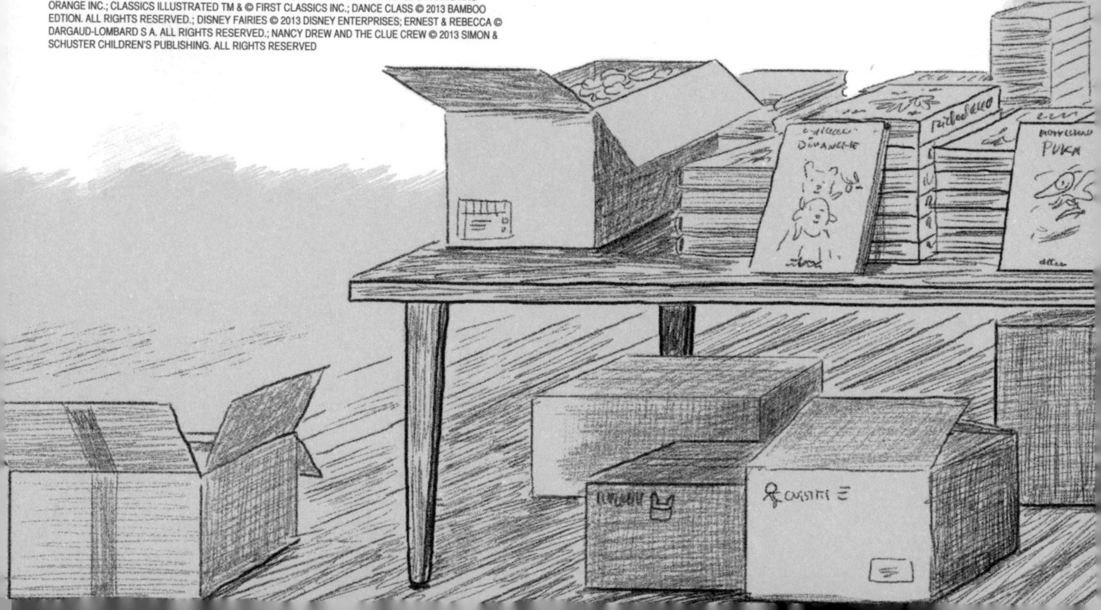

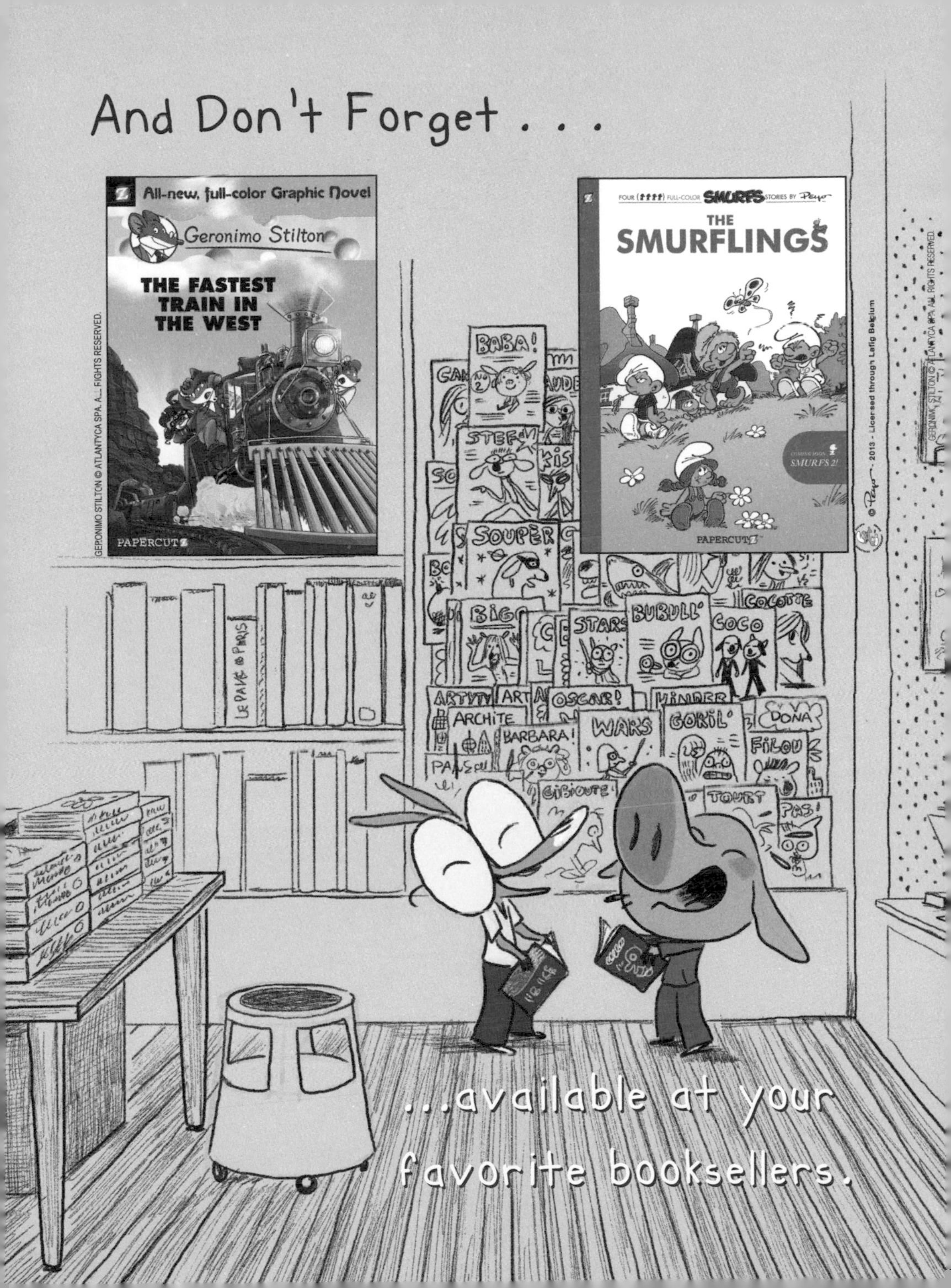
And Don't Forget . . .
All-new, full-color Graphic Novel
Geronimo Stilton
THE FASTEST TRAIN IN THE WEST
PAPERCUTZ
GERONIMO STILTON © ATLANTYCA SPA. ALL RIGHTS RESERVED.
FOUR (4) FULL-COLOR SMURFS STORIES BY Peyo
THE SMURFLINGS
COMING SOON SMURFS 2!
PAPERCUTZ
© Peyo - 2013 - Licensed through Lafig Belgium
...available at your
favorite booksellers.